Lucy Finds Her Way

Other fantastic books in the growing Faithgirlz™ library

BIBLES

The NIV Faithgirlz Bibles

The NKJV Faithgirlz Bible

NIV Faithgirlz Backpack
Bibles

FICTION

**Natalie Grant's
Glimmer Girls Series**

London Art Chase
(Book One)

A Dolphin Wish
(Book Two)

Miracle in Music City
(Book Three)

Light Up New York
(Book Four)

**Samantha Sanderson
Series**

At the Movies (Book One)

On the Scene (Book Two)

Off the Record
(Book Three)

Without a Trace
(Book Four)

Good News Shoes Series

Riley Mae and the
Rock Shocker Trek
(Book One)

Riley Mae and the
Ready Eddy Rapids
(Book Two)

Riley Mae and the
Sole Fire Safari
(Book Three)

The Girls of Harbor View

Girl Power (Book One)

Take Charge (Book Two)

Raising Faith (Book Three)

Secret Admirer
(Book Four)

**Sophie's World Series
(2 books in 1)**

Meet Sophie

Sophie Steps Up

Sophie and Friends

Sophie's Friendship Fiasco

Sophie Flakes Out

Sophie's Drama

The Lucy Series

Lucy Doesn't Wear Pink
(Book One)

Lucy Out of Bounds
(Book Two)

Lucy's "Perfect" Summer
(Book Three)

Lucy Finds Her Way
(Book Four)

From Sadie's Sketchbook

Shades of Truth
(Book One)

Flickering Hope
(Book Two)

Waves of Light
(Book Three)

Brilliant Hues
(Book Four)

NONFICTION

Devotionals

No Boys Allowed

What's a Girl to Do?

Whatever Is Lovely

Shine on, Girl!

That Is So Me

Finding God in Tough
Times

Girl Talk

Girlz Rock

Faithgirlz Bible Studies

The Secret Power of Love

The Secret Power of Joy

The Secret Power of
Goodness

The Secret Power of Grace

Lifestyle and Fun

Faithgirlz Journal

Faithgirlz Cookbook

True You

Best Party Book Ever!

101 Ways to Have Fun

101 Things Every Girl
Should Know

Best Hair Book Ever

Redo Your Room

God's Beautiful Daughter

Everybody Tells Me
to Be Myself but I Don't
Know Who I Am

Check out www.faithgirlz.com

faith*girlz

A LUCY NOVEL

Lucy Finds Her Way

NANCY RUE

ZONDERKIDZ

Lucy Finds Her Way
Copyright © 2009, 2012 by Nancy Rue

This title is also available as a Zondervan ebook. Visit www.zondervan.com/ebooks

Requests for information should be addressed to:
Zondervan, 3900 Sparks Dr. SE, Grand Rapids, Michigan 49546

This edition: ISBN 978-0-310-754527

Library of Congress Cataloging-in-Publication Data

Rue, Nancy-
    Lucy finds her way / by Nancy Rue
      p. cm. — (A Lucy novel ; bk. 4) (Faithgirlz!)
    Summary: As twelve-year-old Lucy prepares for the Olympic Development Program soccer try-outs, she struggles with the complexities of middle school, her relationship with her best friend, and Aunt Karen, who is trying to take over her life while her father is away.
    ISBN 978-0-310-71453-8 (softcover)
    [1. Soccer — Fiction. 2. Middle schools — Fiction. 3. Schools — Fiction. 4. Interpersonal relations — Fiction. 5. Single-parent families — Fiction. 6. Christian life — Fiction. 7. New Mexico — Fiction.] I. Title.
PZ7.R88515Lue   2009
[Fic] — dc22   2009003013

Published in association with the literary agency of Alive Communications, Inc., 7680 Goddard Street, Suite #200, Colorado Springs, CO 80920. www.alivecommunications.com

Zonderkidz is a trademark of Zondervan.

Art direction & cover design: Kris Nelson
Cover illustration: Ria Kim
Interior design: Carlos Eluterio Estrada

Printed in the United States of America

HB 09.25.2020

So we fix our eyes not on what is seen, but on what is unseen,
since what is seen is temporary, but what is unseen is eternal.

— 2 Corinthians 4:18

1

DEAR GOD: WHY I WANT TO CANCEL TODAY.

Lucy pushed the tent of covers aside so she could look at the clock. It was only 6:45 a.m.—plenty of time to make her list. She just wished it were still yesterday or maybe the day before. Any day but the first day of school.

She let the tent-cover fall back over her and Lollipop, the round black ball of a cat, and pressed the pen to the Book of Lists.

1. I have to start middle school. I just got the hang of elementary school, and that took me six years. Middle school is only two years long. I'm in trouble.

2. I won't have Mr. Auggy as my teacher. He's the only one I ever had that didn't think I was stupid. Now I have to start all over with SIX teachers, and everybody says middle school teachers are harder and meaner. I'm losing I.Q. points just thinking about that.

Lollipop gave a nervous meow, and Lucy stopped to scratch the top of her head.

"You don't have to freak out, too, Lolli," she said. "You get to stay home and sleep all day. Lucky."

Lucy gave her another behind-the-ear rub. Actually, she didn't want to sleep. She wanted to play soccer with her team, the Los Suenos Dreams. Or practice in the backyard for the Olympic Development Program tryouts. Or clean the entire house with a toothbrush. Anything but start seventh grade.

"Lucy?" said a sleep-thick voice outside her door. "You're up, aren't you?"

Aunt Karen sounded like she hadn't had her coffee yet. Maybe she'd go back to bed instead of supervising Lucy's wardrobe—

"Leave plenty of time for me to check your outfit," Aunt Karen said. "I don't want you starting middle school looking like a homeless person."

So much for *that* 'maybe.'

"I'm almost ready," Lucy told her. She'd been up for an hour, and she was dressed in what she intended to wear no matter what Aunt Karen said. Which was another thing to add to the list of reasons to cancel the whole day.

3. I want to wear my jeans and my Los Suenos Dreams t-shirt — which is the same as J.J. is gonna wear — and I bet Aunt Karen already has something pink and pleated picked out. One of the sixteen she bought me at the mall in Las Cruces after twenty hours of shopping. There's gonna be a fight.

4. And Dad isn't here to be on my side.

Lucy scooted further under her tent. That was the biggest reason of all for canceling the day. If her dad was here at home, instead of off in Albuquerque at the School for the Blind learning technological stuff so he could keep his job at the radio station—Lucy took a big breath from that thought. If he were here, he wouldn't let Aunt Karen make her be all girly when that was *so* not her. He would say, "Leave her alone, K. She looks beautiful to me." And Lucy would grin—because, of course, being blind, Dad couldn't see her at all. She liked being the kind of beautiful you can't see.

Lucy closed the Book of Lists and ran her fingers across the raised leaves on the green cover. It would be even better if her mom were here, instead of just the book she'd left behind. Her mom would wear jeans and t-shirts, too, and would go *with* her to meet all her teachers and let them know that Lucy would read or write anything they wanted her to as long as it had something to do with soccer. Her mom would show her how to be a girl in seventh grade.

But Mom wasn't here. Some days, it didn't hurt so much having a mom who had died. Today wasn't one of those days.

"I don't hear you moving around in there," Aunt Karen said out in the hall. The doorknob wiggled, but Lucy had it locked. Dad told Aunt Karen before he left that Lucy needed her privacy and was allowed to lock her door. That was only one of the reasons he was the coolest dad on the planet.

"I'm moving," Lucy said.

She threw back the covers and climbed out of bed and carefully tucked the Book of Lists under her pillow. The only people who knew about the Book were Dad and Inez and Mora and J.J.—and none of them had read it. Aunt Karen suspected Lucy had it—and if she ever found it, she'd take it away—she'd said that before. She said it had belonged to her sister, Lucy's mom, and she thought it ought to be put in a museum or something because Mom was a famous reporter who was killed in the war in Iraq.

"But it's mine, right, Lolli?" Lucy said to the kitty. "Keep it safe."

Lolli settled on top of the pillow and winked herself back to sleep. Lucy had to count on her. Without the Book she didn't know if she could figure out just how to be a girl. It was a very hard thing without a mom.

Lucy then straightened the red and blue letters on her white t-shirt so Aunt Karen wouldn't make her iron it, and rested her arms on her windowsill. Still no sign of her best friend J.J., peeking out of the sheet he used for a curtain over his window across the street. He always rode bikes to school with her, but she wasn't really surprised that he wasn't out yet. He was even less excited about starting middle school than she was. At least his mom wouldn't be inspecting his outfit. He only had about three to choose from anyway.

"I'm fixing your breakfast," Aunt Karen called from the kitchen.

Lucy forced herself not to roll her eyes when she opened the door. Dad had made her promise not to pull any "attitude" with Aunt Karen. That meant no eye-rolling, heavy sighing, get-out-my-face tone of voice, shrugging instead of answering, or slamming of doors.

"Think you can handle that, Champ?" Dad had said to her.

"As long as it's only for six weeks," Lucy told him.

So far she hadn't slammed or rolled or sighed. But, then, they were only a half a week into Aunt Karen's stay.

Lucy didn't ride the yellow Navajo rug down the tile hall to the kitchen the way she usually did. She wasn't, after all, that eager to get there. When she did, she found Aunt Karen in white sweats—who wore *white* hang-out clothes?—and her hair in a falling-down ponytail, staring into the refrigerator.

"I can fix my own breakfast," Lucy said.

"You're not going off with a Pop Tart," Aunt Karen said. "I'm making you scrambled eggs."

Lucy resisted the urge to push her aunt into the refrigerator and went for the pantry. "I always have cereal."

"Negative. I've seen the cereal collection in this house."

Lucy didn't like it when Aunt Karen referred to the *home* she and Dad shared as "this house"—as if it was some sort of shack without electricity. She pulled a box of Captain Crunch from the shelf and turned around to find Aunt Karen with her arms folded and an eleven pinched into the skin between her eyebrows. She was licking her lips the way she did at least a dozen times a day.

"I thought you said you were dressed," she said.

"I am," Lucy said.

"What about those cute clothes I bought you?"

"I have soccer practice right after school. I'd get them dirty." Lucy avoided her aunt's eyes as she pulled aside the red and white checked curtain that served as a cabinet door and slid out a bowl. It was a good thing she couldn't slam that. As Aunt Karen jerked a container of skim milk out of the refrigerator and smacked it onto the table, Lucy wished Dad had given *her* some attitude rules.

"Do you have any idea what kind of impression you're going to make on your new teachers wearing that get-up?" Aunt Karen said.

Lucy maneuvered around her to get the whole milk out of the refrigerator. "I'm clean and I don't have an attitude," she said. She moved Marmalade, the orange kitty who liked Dad best, off of the chair and sat down. "That's a good enough impression."

"Your clothes *are* your attitude." Aunt Karen's long-comma eyebrows went up as she watched Lucy dump Captain Crunch into the bowl and drown it in almost-cream. "Jeans and a t-shirt say you don't care about your appearance, which sends the message that you don't care what people think."

"I *don't* care what people think," Lucy said, mouth full. "Well, not all people."

"At least let me do your hair." Aunt Karen miraculously pulled a brush out of the pocket of her sweatshirt. "You always wear it in a French braid for soccer anyway."

Lucy couldn't argue with that, and it would be kind of hard for her to fight off Aunt Karen while she was trying to eat. Although it was also hard to chew when her temples were being pulled to the back of her head.

"I bet your girlfriends won't show up in last year's jeans," Aunt Karen said as she dragged the brush through Lucy's thick blonde hair. "Dusty and Vanessa—"

"Veronica," Lucy said. "I know. They like clothes."

"You don't want to be like them? They're such cool girls."

She didn't say, "And they could teach you how to be cool, too," but Lucy knew she was thinking it.

"My friends don't expect me to be like them," Lucy said. "They like me because I'm just who I am."

"Okay, listen to me." Aunt Karen produced a blue hair elastic. "That works in elementary school, but, trust me, it all changes in middle school. Right or wrong, the *only* thing that matters once you hit seventh grade is being part of the crowd. You can be all independent and march to the beat of a different drummer if you want to, but I'm here to tell you, you're only going to wind up by yourself if you do that."

"Are you done?"

"Excuse me?"

"With my hair. Are you done?"

"Yes, and it's cute. Go look in the mirror."

Lucy escaped to the bathroom, leaving Marmalade and Artemis Hamm, their hunter cat, to fight over what was left in her bowl, and after an eye-rolling glance in the mirror she brushed her teeth until she was pretty sure the enamel was going to come off. How was she going to stand this for five and a half more weeks?

"J.J.'s outside waiting for you," Aunt Karen called to her. *That* was how she was going to stand it. Lucy did a final spit, snatched her backpack and net soccer ball bag from the hook by the back door, and gave Aunt Karen a quick wave.

"Let me just say this before you go, "Aunt Karen said.

But the phone rang and Lucy dove for the door.

Aunt Karen looked at the caller I.D. and put up a finger. "It's your father. Don't you want to talk to him?"

Lucy snatched the phone from her hand and slipped out the back door with it.

"Dad?" she said.

"Hey, Champ! Happy first day of school."

"Very funny."

Dad laughed his sand-in-a-bucket laugh, and Lucy could almost imagine the light that poured out of him whenever he smiled, and smell his breath-mint-tweedy-jacket smell. It made her want to see him. Bad.

"Can you look at it as an adventure?" he said. "This is going to be a whole new experience for you."

I don't want a whole new experience, she almost said to him. *I want things back the way they were.*

But she didn't say it—because if Dad knew how scared she was, he might come home right now. And then he would lose his job. And that would be her fault.

"Yeah," she said instead. "Regular classes now and not the dumb group."

"That's one way to put it." Dad's voice went soft. "Luce—there's no need to be nervous. You worked with Mr. Auggy all summer. You passed the standardized reading test. You're way up into seventh grade reading level."

"I know," Lucy said. "How are *your* classes going?"

"Whew." Dad chuckled. "It's been a long time since I went to school. I'm way out of practice." He chuckled. "Maybe you could give me a few pointers after today, huh?"

"Sure," Lucy said.

And then she wished he was going to be there to talk about it at supper over Inez's enchiladas, with Marmalade the kitty in his lap and the sunlight smile on his face.

But she swallowed hard as she turned off the phone and went back inside to hang it up. She couldn't start bawling now. She didn't know that much about middle school, but she was pretty sure people didn't cry there.

Especially not Lucy Rooney.

It helped that J.J. was waiting outside the gate. Although he was glaring at Mudge, the Rooneys' fourth kitty, who was glaring back from under the century plant, he still made Lucy almost smile. With his Apache-black ponytail hanging from the nape of his neck and his lanky legs ready to be tripped over the minute he took a step, he looked the same as he always did. At least there was that.

"Where's Januarie?" Lucy said.

"Home."

"Why?"

"Elementary starts later."

"Oh, yeah."

"The only thing good about middle school—"

"Is that Januarie's not there," Lucy finished for him.

Those were two more things that hadn't changed: J.J.'s nine year old sister was still at Los Suenos Elementary, and J.J. still thought she was a moron. Januarie bugged Lucy, too, but Lucy didn't have to put up with her Chihuahua voice twenty-four/seven like J.J. did. Even though she wasn't quite as whiny as she used to be, now that State Children's Services wouldn't let J.J.'s father live with them anymore because he was in a lot of trouble with the law, Januarie continued to drive J.J. nuts whenever she got the chance.

13

J.J. already had one long leg flung over his bike and Lucy was climbing onto the new one she'd just gotten for her birthday when she heard a loud "Yo, Lucy Goosey," from the corner of First and Granada Streets. She knew it was Gabe Navarra before she even turned around. He *hadn't* stayed the same since they finished sixth grade. His voice had dipped into man-zone and he even had some dark fuzz on his chocolate-colored chin. Lucy figured since his dad was the sheriff, he had to skip right from boy to tough guy.

Gabe ambled up to them with tall Emanuel Ramos on one side and short, square Oscar Mozingo on the other, like bookends that didn't match. A giggle behind them meant Veronica DeMatteo was there, too, and if she was, so was Dusty Terricola. The whole Los Suenos Dreams team surrounded her, except for Carla Rosa, and Lucy broke into the first grin she'd managed that morning.

The two girls scurried, still giggling, around the guys, Dusty shoving Oscar before he could shove her and laughing into his face with a smile that crinkled her hot-chocolate-creamy skin. Veronica, however, was not amused. She stood with her mouth hanging slightly open, as usual, staring at Lucy and J.J. out of her caramel-colored face.

"What?" Lucy said.

"You aren't riding your *bikes*, are you?"

Lucy looked at J.J., who just looked back with his too-blue eyes.

"We always do," Lucy said.

Veronica put up both hands and waved them like she was erasing the very thought.

"What?" Lucy said again.

Dusty tossed back her Hispanic-black hair and put a hand on Lucy's arm. "Nobody rides their bikes to middle school, *Bolillo*."

Even though Dusty used the nickname Lucy liked—which meant she wasn't Hispanic or Native American but she was okay anyway—Lucy felt suddenly prickly.

"Why not?" she said.

"Because it ain't cool," Oscar said.

Gabe gave Oscar's head a push. "Like you'd know what cool was if it spit in your eye."

14

"I don't care about being cool," Lucy said. "I just care about getting to school."

"Guess what?"

They all turned to the roundish figure with its cloud of red hair chugging toward them. Carla Rosa's face was crimson, and it wasn't even that hot yet. That happened when she was jittery. That and the constant "guess whats."

"Guess what?" she said again.

"What?" they all said—because if they didn't, she'd keep on until somebody did.

"There aren't any bike racks at the middle school," she said.

"Are so," J.J. mumbled.

Carla Rosa shook the curls. "My dad said—guess what, he's the mayor—"

"We *know*," Veronica said. She twitched her thin, brown ponytail so hard it almost smacked Gabe in the face.

"They took them all down because nobody rides bikes to middle school."

Gabe leaned toward Lucy and said in a loud, deep whisper, "Because it ain't cool, Lucy Goosey."

"Just walk with us, *'lillo*," Dusty said. "It'll be more fun anyway."

Lucy did not get it. At all. But she and J.J. left their bikes in her back yard and joined the walking group to amble across the street to the white adobe middle school, standing stark and stern against the Sacramento Mountains that always made Lucy think of protective uncles. Today they weren't doing such a good job, as far as she was concerned.

And the team's idea of 'fun' didn't match Lucy's right now, either. All anybody could talk about was how much harder and meaner the teachers were going to be and how impossible it would be to remember your locker combination and still get to class on time and how all the eighth graders were going to make their lives miserable. By the time they pushed through the big glass front doors, Lucy's entire stomach was like a bowl of knotted up spaghetti.

15

"But it's still going to be awesome," Dusty said.

Lucy looked around at the herd pushing its way down the hall and listened to the squawking intercom that told them all to get to first period and smelled the perfume of a passing bevy of thirteen year old girls and wondered how it was possibly going to be awesome. Girls were wearing *perfume?*

Lucy, Dusty, Veronica, Gabe, and J.J. said good-bye to Carla Rosa and Oscar and Emanuel, who were in a different class, and Lucy tried not to cling to Dusty as they wove their way through the mob to Room 101. At least she was with some of her team. And at least they all, except for Gabe, of course, looked almost as ready to throw up their Captain Crunch as she was.

But Lucy was only five minutes into the first class before she knew her team wasn't going to be able to help her with Mrs. Huntington, the English teacher who lectured them on commas and semi-colons, whatever they were.

Or with the second period social studies instructor, Mr. Lopez, who gave them ten pounds of homework to lug in their backpacks.

Or with Mrs. Marks, the science lady whose voice was a cure for insomnia; Veronica had to poke Gabe twice to keep him from nodding off.

And they were going to be no help at all with the study hall monitor, that was for sure. She was the worst one of all.

Lucy followed the flock into her big cavern of a room fourth period and dumped her backpack and her soccer ball bag onto the table the frizzy-haired lady pointed her to.

"Athletic equipment is not allowed in here," the lady said—in a voice deeper than Gabe's. Lucy had to look at her closely to make sure she was, indeed, a female.

Frizzy Lady looked closely right back. "*No equipo en la clase.*"

"She doesn't speak Spanish," Dusty said.

"Then what *does* she speak?"

"English," Veronica said.

"So far I haven't heard her speak at all. Which doesn't matter, as long as she understands what I'm saying." The teacher's deep voice got louder. "No athletic equipment in here," she said again, and picked up Lucy's soccer ball bag and hauled it to the front of the long room where she dropped it on a table. As she turned to corral the rest of the class in the door, the ball, bag and all, rolled to the floor. Several kids laughed. Lucy felt her face burn like she was standing over a campfire.

"Excuse me?" she said.

The lady just kept pointing people to tables.

"Excuse me," Lucy said again.

"Leave it alone," J.J. muttered at her elbow.

But Lucy stitched her way through the students still getting to their places and stood next to Frizzy Lady.

"Am I going to get my ball back?" she said.

The teacher closed the door and folded her arms over a chest that seemed too big for the rest of her.

"I don't know what you're going to do with it if you do," she said. "You aren't getting a locker until tomorrow and since you don't appear to have gotten the memo, there are no Physical Education classes for seventh graders."

Lucy knew. She hadn't gotten a "memo," but Carla Rosa had already guess-whatted her about it. She also knew there was only one girls' sport at Los Suenos Middle and that was softball in the spring, which meant the Dreams had to keep going on their own. So when Frizzy Lady nodded Lucy toward her table, she didn't move yet.

"I'll need my ball for lunch," she said.

"I'd suggest a sandwich, myself."

The entire class, so shy moments before, burst into a giant guffaw. Lucy was sure her own face had fallen *into* the campfire.

"I wasn't planning to eat it," she said, trying very hard to keep the attitude out of her voice. "My team and I were going to practice."

That made the class roar again. Dusty tugged at Lucy's sleeve and pulled her back to their table, while Frizzy Lady put her hand in the air.

"All right, people," she said, "this is a study hall, which means you're here to study. And I suggest some of you–" She looked right at Lucy. "—study the school handbook. For starters, folks, you aren't on the playground any more."

Once again the class showed their appreciation with hissing laughs and rolling eyes and what felt like a pulling-together into a private joke.

A joke Lucy didn't get.

2

At the end of fourth period study hall, Lucy snatched her ball in its bag and escaped from the room while Dusty and Veronica cornered Frizzy Lady—whose name, she finally told them, was Ms. Pasqual—and distracted her with questions about stuff they already knew.

When they were settled in the cafeteria, Lucy stuffed the bag under the table when they were settled in the cafeteria, but that didn't keep a dimpled girl with braces from stopping by with her friend who looked exactly like her to say, "Oh, so you're *not* eating your soccer ball."

"No," Lucy said to them. "I forgot to bring salsa, and I won't eat it without salsa."

They didn't crack a smile, even though Lucy thought it was a whole lot funnier than anything Frizzy Lady had said.

"Evil," Veronica said when they were gone.

"But hot," Gabe said, wiggling his eyebrows.

"Shut up," Dusty told him.

No one buzzed her, like they would have done back when they were with Mr. Auggy. Every time they told each other to shut up or did something else hateful, he would give them a loud BUZZ. When they did something that showed integrity, like sticking up for each other, they got a DING-DING-DING. Lucy didn't think there would be a whole lot of ding-ding-dinging around here, either.

"What are *they* doing?" Carla Rosa said.

Lucy followed her pointing finger to a line of boys she sort of recognized from her classes. They were standing behind one of the tables, fists in the air, eyes on the milk carton each had on the table top below him. One of the dimply girls with the braces was up on one knee in a chair, counting down from ten.

"Oh, nuh–uh," Dusty said.

"What?" Veronica said.

"They are *so* going to smash those milk cartons with their fists."

"Guess what?" Carla Rosa said. "They're going to get in trouble."

Lucy grunted. "Especially since the cartons are full."

Gabe stood up, grinning like a chimpanzee. "I hope they are, dude. That would be cool."

Just as the girl with the braces reached a loud, giggling, "Two!" Frizzy Lady descended on the table and all the fists disappeared behind backs.

"I told you they were going to get in trouble," Carla Rosa said.

But it didn't look to Lucy like they did. Frizzy Lady just made them sit back in their chairs and moved on to the next "cool" thing that was happening three tables down. It looked like an olive spitting contest.

Lucy glanced at her watch. "How much time do we have?"

"Twenty-three minutes," Dusty said.°

"No, seriously," Lucy said.

"Guess what, she's right." Carla Rosa nodded until the curls on top of her head bounced. The ones at the sides stuck to her cheeks like she'd been sweating all morning.

Lucy popped the plastic top back on the salad Aunt Karen had packed for her, which she didn't want anyway. Dad had always made her a peanut butter and pickle sandwich on days that were going to be hard.

"I'm done," she said. "Are you guys ready?"

Veronica's lower lip hung. "Ready for what?"

"For soccer practice. We don't have that much time, but we could at least—" Lucy looked around the table at faces that didn't look at her. "What?" she said.

"Am I gonna have to give you Cool Lessons this whole year?" Gabe said. "You don't ride your bike to middle school and you don't play soccer during lunch." He swept his sparkly-dark eyes over the crowded lunchroom. "You figure out who's hot and who's not."

"You disgust me," Veronica said.

"Tell me you ain't done a hottie check," Oscar said to her.

When she told him to shut up and no one buzzed, Lucy turned to Dusty.

"Don't you want to practice?" Lucy said to her.

Dusty kept her eyes on the small bag of Doritos she was eating daintily out of. "No offense, *Bolillo*, but I don't really want to get teased like you just did. I mean, they laughed because you brought a ball to school. What do you think they're going to do if we go outside and start dribbling one?"

"Guess what? Me too," Carla said. "I already got called a retard today."

Gabe snickered. "Well, you—"

"Shut up," J.J. said.

Dusty put her hand on Lucy's arm. "We'll still practice after school at the field, okay?"

Veronica turned from smacking Oscar for something long enough to say, "Mr. Auggy will be there, so nobody can be mean to us."

"I don't care if they're mean!" Lucy said.

"Me neither." Gabe got up from the table and did a weird jerky thing with his head toward the milk carton crew. "But lunch is the time for hangin' out and bein' cool, and I'm gonna go do it."

"Not without me," said Veronica, who claimed Gabe as hers no matter what stupid boy thing he did or said.

Dusty stood up, too. "We better go stake out our territory before all the good hanging-out spots are taken. You guys coming?"

J.J. shrugged and looked at Lucy. She wasn't sure how to hang out, and she obviously didn't know anything about being cool. All she wanted to do was kick a soccer ball and run after it and feel the way that always made her feel, which was better than how she felt right now.

"Okay," she said to Dusty.

But by the time they located a low wall in the courtyard where everybody could sit and hang their legs, the bell rang and everybody scattered to fifth period. Lucy stuffed the ball in her backpack and trudged toward the Life Skills room.

"Who are you, the Hunchback?" a kid with a greasy face said to her in the hall.

"Hey, Quasimodo!" said his equally oily buddy.

"Ignore them," Dusty whispered to Lucy.

"Yeah, but you know what?" Veronica said. "They could be talking to any of the three of us because we're the only girls with backpacks. Everybody else has one of those cute messenger bags." Her big eyes were somber. "I'm so making my mom take me to Alamogordo tonight to get me one at Wal-Mart."

"I wanna come," Dusty said.

"You totally can."

They both looked at Lucy.

"This backpack's fine," she said.

"You're so secure, '*lillo*," Dusty said.

Lucy had no idea what that had to do with backpacks.

Or what the list of skills they were going to learn in fifth period had to do with life. At least her life.

She stared down at the hand-out Mr. Torres gave them, about values and relationships and managing money, and wondered if he was as bored with it as he sounded and as the class seemed to be. Maybe they were all feeling cooler after hanging out at lunch, because several kids weren't as scared-acting as they'd been during morning classes.

Lucy saw the two look-alike girls Veronica had dubbed as "evil" passing a note back and forth and caught two guys making spit wads which they hoarded inside their desks. One girl was even sending a text message on the phone she wasn't supposed to have. Lucy *had* gotten that memo, not that it mattered because she and dad didn't have cell phones—or a computer—or even cable.

But judging from the amount of attention Mr. Torres was actually paying them, she could have used all three in this class and gotten away with it. Everybody else seemed to have picked up on that too, because while he droned on about how they were going to learn to manage their time, more cell phones came out of pockets and more kids without them resorted to sending messages the old fashioned way and the spit wads were pelted across the room. One hit Gabe right in the temple. He picked it up and stuck it in his ear, which broke the second row completely up. Even then Mr. Torres only glanced their way and said, "I'm glad to see you people are still awake."

How was anybody supposed to sleep with all this going on?

Lucy turned the sheet over and drew a diagram of a soccer field. This was a good time to work out some new strategies. She'd barely gotten the first X placed when a folded piece of paper landed on her desk. She looked around, but nobody was looking at her, so it had to be a mistaken delivery.

Except that her name was printed on it, and it didn't look like Dusty or Veronica's handwriting. Besides, they were both looking over the shoulder of the girl in front of them, whose text messaging thumbs were going so fast you could hardly see them.

Lucy unfolded the note, and felt her eyes bulge.

CONGRATULATIONS!!! YOU HAVE BEEN NAMED THE CLASS WEIRDO!!!

Lucy forced herself not to look up and ask, "Who resigned and left this person in charge of who's weird and who's not?"

Like this was news anyway. Of course she was a weirdo. She didn't care what kind of backpack she carried or whether people thought she ate her soccer ball for lunch. It didn't take a rocket scientist to figure out that made a person different. She had that down and the first day of middle school wasn't even over.

She just sure wished it would be.

But there was one more period to go, and Lucy could hardly drag herself to Room 111 for pre-algebra. J.J. walked with her, dragging his too-big-for-him feet.

"I hate math," he said.

"I know," Lucy said, even though it was the one subject she actually didn't stink at.

"Let's leave."

"We can't."

"Why?"

"You'll get in trouble with Winnie the State Lady."

"So?"

"So—it doesn't matter how nice she is to you and how much she wants you and your mom to stay together, she'll put you in foster care if she thinks you're out of control."

J.J. grunted as they crossed into Room 111. "It might be better than this."

The Team found the only table that was left, right in the front of the room in the center. Other kids snickered and probably would have whispered something about them being Brainers or Teachers' Pets, Lucy knew, if Gabe hadn't been with them. He'd been raising *his* cool factor all afternoon.

When the bell rang, a big man with very-short gray hair—which was so flat on top he could have carried a tray of sodas on it—closed the door and put his hands on his hips and looked at the class with small hard eyes. At the table behind them, a guy said, "At-ten-SHUN!" and some girls laughed.

The teacher didn't. He said, "The only person calling anyone to attention here will be me." He scanned the room and drained it of its cocky fifth period attitude. Lucy could feel everybody getting terrified again.

"I'm Mr. Vick," he said. "My students call me Colonel."

Lucy doubted anybody would call him anything else.

"I'm going to teach you pre-algebra," he said, "and you're going to learn it. Nobody fails my class." He gave them his commanding look again. "Nobody."

Lucy heard J.J. swallow. She saw Dusty and Veronica grow small in their chairs. She watched Gabe decide to hold back any smart remarks until he figured out how to get around this guy.

Lucy just opened her notebook and took out her pencil. What was there to figure out? You didn't mess with the Colonel.

At least there was one thing about middle school that made sense.

3

When the last bell finally rang, Lucy thought two weeks must have gone by since first period. The class filed silently out of the Colonel's room, but she didn't wait around to join in the, "Can you *believe* that dude?" conversation in the hall. With a "See you there in thirty minutes!" called over her shoulder to her team, she headed for home.

She would have gone straight to their soccer field, except that she always checked in with Inez first. At least Aunt Karen's car wasn't at the house, which meant she was probably out shopping.

Lucy could never figure out what there could possibly be to buy that required so many trips to the Alamogordo Wal-Mart and the mall in Las Cruces and the fancy little shops at Ruidoso where Lucy always managed to knock something over. She was grateful now, however. She hoped Aunt Karen's shopping spree would last into tomorrow.

Inez was in the kitchen where she always was when Lucy came home from school, fixing *sopapillas* to fill with honey or *quesadillas* she could dip in salsa. The snack was ready, but Inez's usual greeting wasn't. The eyes beneath her straight cut bangs were dark and moody looking.

"*Buenos tardes, Senorita Lucy,*" she said in a voice squeezed out between her teeth.

Lucy said hi and slipped into a chair at the table across from Inez's granddaughter, Mora.

What's up with her? Lucy asked with her eyes.

Mora reached for her cell phone, which was never far from her finger tips, and then frowned.

"I forgot you don't *have* a phone," she said, rolling her huge brown eyes. "I can't text you."

Inez set a bowl of her homemade tortilla chips on the table and rustled out of the room.

"You could try just *telling* me," Lucy whispered.

Mora leaned in. Her eyes were now shining as she flipped her fudge-colored hair over her shoulders. She loved being the bearer of news, especially if it was bad.

"*Abuela* is mad at your Aunt Karen," Mora said.

"Why?" Lucy said.

Mora plucked a chip from the bright blue bowl. "You know how *Abuela* always grocery shops for your dad at Mr. Benitez's store?"

"Uh-huh."

"Well, your aunt said his food isn't that good and she was going to the Wal-Mart in Alamogordo and buying it."

Lucy wasn't quite sure why that would make Inez mad, though she could imagine Aunt Karen saying it like Inez didn't know anything because she didn't wear lip gloss or walk around with a cell phone hanging in her ear.

"My dad will make her stop," Lucy said. "He wants us to buy from the stores here so they don't go out of business."

"Whatever." Mora sloshed a chip up and down in the salsa. "They didn't have a big fight or anything, but Abuela stopped talking after Aunt Karen left, which means she's mad." She gave the eyes another roll. "I wish she'd stop talking when she's mad at *me.*"

Like that was going to happen. Mora was in trouble with her grandmother at least once a day for something, and she got a lecture in Spanish every time.

Mora leaned back in her chair and threw her arms over her head like she was about to make a big announcement. "So — do you totally love middle school or what? I mean, mine in Alamogordo is so much better than elementary school I can't even believe it. We were such babies last year. And there are *so* many more cute boys now. They're, like, all over the place. I was tripping over them!"

Her fingers punctuated the air as if she were making commas and periods and exclamation points, which Lucy usually found pretty funny. This time, though, she abandoned the chips and picked up her soccer ball bag.

"Will you tell Inez I went to practice?" she said.

"Hello! We're talking here!"

Lucy didn't point out that *Mora* was the only one talking, and could probably carry on the whole conversation without Lucy even being there. She couldn't deal with that today. She had to get to the soccer field and see if she was still the same person she'd been when she woke up that morning: Cheryl Rooney's daughter with her exactly sixteen freckles and her talent for soccer and her own way of being a girl. Whatever that was.

Before Lucy even got across Highway 54 and over the new-since-the-flood bridge and down a dirt road, she decided maybe she was. The air was crisp and laced with sunshine that glinted on the leaves of the cottonwoods and made them look like gold coins. Some of them fluttered across her path as she rode her bike toward the place she loved most in the whole town. The place where she was her best self.

Unfortunately, the soccer field wasn't *its* best self right now. J.J.'s father had destroyed the refreshment building and turned the bleachers into a pile of toothpicks last summer and tried to make it look like a storm had done it. Some people in Los Suenos said they should just give up and let a big corporation buy the land from the town and build a gas station and Mini-Mart there. The town that had been pulled together by the soccer team last winter was once more divided in half.

But when Lucy arrived at the field, Mr. Auggy was smiling his small smile as he watched the team put on their cleats and their shin guards and listened to Carla Rosa's 'guess-whats'. It didn't seem to matter to him that the field was a shambles and the shopkeepers were fighting. Lucy was once again absolutely sure she was still Lucy Rooney of the Los Suenos Dreams soccer team, and not just the Seventh Grade Class Weirdo.

"There's our Captain," Mr. Auggy said. His small smile got bigger. "I missed you guys today."

Januarie raised a pudgy hand. "Except me. You saw me."

"You're hard to miss," J.J. muttered.

For once, Lucy was a little envious of Januarie, getting to be with Mr. Auggy all day and not having to deal with the cool factor. That passed quickly, though, as Januarie's nine-year-old voice went up into its Chihuahua whine.

"But there was nobody to play soccer with at recess!" she wailed.

"Join the club," Lucy said.

Mr. Auggy tilted his head at her, his shiny shock of light brown hair sliding across his forehead. "You didn't practice at lunchtime?" he said.

"We barely got time to eat," Oscar said.

Lucy looked around, but nobody was telling Mr. Auggy that it wasn't cool to play soccer when everybody else was hanging out. One more thing Lucy just didn't get.

"Then I guess we're going to have to make up for that," Mr. Auggy said. "I'm trying to schedule a game for you—as long as you don't mind playing on someone else's field."

"I'm cool with that," Gabe said.

So was Lucy. After what she'd seen that day, she was glad there wasn't enough money for the county to have a school-sponsored team. She couldn't imagine any of her teachers caring about her getting into the Olympic Development Program the way Mr. Auggy did. It was a huge deal you had to be picked for so you could get ready to go for the real Olympics, and she had already gotten past one hurdle. She was itching to get to the next one.

Mr. Auggy reached for the ball of bags. "Then let's warm up with a little juggling."

It only took a few attempts at trying to keep her ball in the air longer than J.J. to put Lucy in soccer zone. Soccer ball juggling contests, and playing defenders-and-attackers and making more points than Gabe's side, and even enduring being called Lucy Goosey by him in Soccer Red Rover—all of that made her grin from one ear lobe to the other, until she was sure her smile met at the back of her head.

Even when Mr. Auggy was calling out instructions—"Watch the

ball, not your opponent!" "Your arms are off limits! No pushing!" "Keep the ball close to your feet! Stay in control of it!"—even then, it warmed Lucy as if he were saying, "Come over and hang out with me! I want to be best friends!" She was zinging.

Until Mr. Auggy called for a water break, and Lucy saw a familiar figure standing at the touchline with a cooler. She knew who it was, but she still shielded her eyes with her hand and squinted, in hopes that she was wrong.

She wasn't.

"Lucy, that's your aunt," Veronica said, voice wistful like she was window-shopping. "She's so cool."

She darted off toward Aunt Karen with Dusty and Carla Rosa right behind her. Why was it that every other girl in the universe liked Aunt Karen except her?

Probably because Aunt Karen didn't try to do Extreme Makeovers on *them*—although Lucy *had* heard her murmur that she'd like to go after Carla Rosa's hair with a flat iron.

"This is a surprise, Ms. Crosslin," Mr. Auggy was saying to her when Lucy joined the group.

Aunt Karen, who was crouched by the cooler, flashed a smile up at him, and Lucy saw Veronica poke Dusty. That meant she thought Aunt Karen had a crush on Mr. Auggy. Ewwww.

"Aren't soccer moms supposed to bring a wholesome snack for the team?" Aunt Karen said.

Soccer moms? Wholesome snack?

Lucy heard Gabe snicker under his breath. Oscar didn't even try to smother a snort.

"Guess what?" Carla Rosa said. "That's why Januarie's here—and she just gives us water."

"And not enough as far as I can tell." Aunt Karen stood up with water bottles dangling between her fingers. "Januarie, give them each one of these, and then they can each have a juice box."

"Oh, goody!" Gabe said in a high-pitched voice.

Mr. Auggy didn't buzz him, but he did give him a look.

"Look what else she has!" Januarie said. She was peering into the cooler. "There's string cheese—and candy bars!"

"*Protein* bars," Aunt Karen said. "Our team is going to get a nutritious boost. You have to keep your energy up."

Lucy didn't need energy, not if she was just going to die of embarrassment anyway. Gabe and Oscar and even Emanuel's faces were brilliant red from the jeers they were holding back. Dusty and Veronica wore plastic smiles. J.J. looked like he was just glad she wasn't *his* aunt. The only person who didn't seem to think Aunt Karen was acting like they were on a kindergarten field trip was Januarie. Of course. There was food involved.

"Oh, my *gosh!*"

Everyone came out of their various states of disbelief to look at Aunt Karen, who was holding Carla Rosa's arm and staring at it.

"What's up?" Mr. Auggy said.

"Look at this child's skin!"

"Eww—what's wrong with it?" Januarie said.

"Be quiet, moron," J.J. told her.

No one buzzed. They were intent on Aunt Karen, shaking her head over Carla Rosa's forearm. She looked up at Mr. Auggy.

"Don't you make them wear sunscreen?" she said. "This child's skin is super-sensitive."

"Guess what? My name's Carla."

"She's a prime candidate for skin cancer."

"Gross," Oscar said.

Aunt Karen scanned the group with her eyes, while Lucy wished the bleachers hadn't fallen down so she could crawl under them.

"I know you think darker skin isn't susceptible, but even you Hispanic types need to be careful." She stuck a hand into her bag, without taking her eyes off of the team, and produced not one but two tubes. "SPF 15 for the Latinos," she said. "Lucy, you and Carol, was it?—you two need the 45."

Lucy decided she might crawl under those piles of wood after all.

"What about me?" Januarie said, sticking out her arm. "I'm Apache. So's J.J."

"But don't you have a white father?" Aunt Karen said.

"We don't have a father at all," J.J. mumbled.

Lucy was sure only she had heard it. She was also sure no SPF of any number was going on his skin. Not the way he was backing up and clamping down his jaw. Those were clear J.J. signals for, "Get off me."

"You know what, team?" Mr. Auggy said. "I think you ought to thank Ms. Crosslin for coming out. And then I think we're just about done for today."

Lucy was *definitely* done. Still wearing her cleats and shin guards, she grabbed her ball and bolted for her bike with J.J. practically climbing up her calves.

"I'm not doin' that," J.J. said, only after they'd crossed the bridge.

"I know," Lucy said.

"Are you gonna?"

"Have we met? No, I'm not wearing her stupid sunscreen."

Or eating a wholesome snack or drinking out of a juice box or sticking around to find out what other plans Aunt Karen had for totally ruining their soccer team. Lucy bet right that very minute she was telling Mr. Auggy they should all have their nails done before their next game.

J.J. stopped at Highway 54 and looked over at Lucy, who pulled up beside him.

"At least my mom leaves me alone," he said.

"Hello! My Aunt Karen's not my mom!"

"How much longer?"

"Five and a half weeks."

"Too long."

Lucy just nodded. Yeah, it was waaay too long.

But she didn't tell Dad that when he called right after she got home, before Aunt Karen arrived with her cooler. He wanted to hear all about her day, and it was hard enough to hide an attitude just talking about middle school. It would be impossible if she got into the scene at the soccer field. As she carried the phone and her soccer ball out to the back yard, Lucy scrambled around in her brain for something good to tell him.

"The math teacher's interesting," she said as she stepped over the ball to practice her inside turn. "He says to call him Colonel."

Dad chuckled. "That must be Mr. Vick. He calls into the station sometimes. Great guy."

Lucy's throat felt thick. If only Dad were at the station right now, chatting away with the Colonel over the radio . . .

"So what else, Luce?" Dad said.

She used the inside of her foot to push the ball backwards. "Well, I was given a title."

"Oh?"

"Yeah. Class Weirdo."

"Is that a good thing or a bad thing?"

"I guess they think it's a bad thing." She stepped over the ball again. "I'm okay with it, though. At least I don't have to wear one of those sash things, so there's that."

He laughed his sandpapery laugh again. "That's my Champ. How are things on the A.K. front?"

She trapped the ball and stopped. "You know what she did, Dad?" she started to say.

But outside the gate, Mudge growled under his kitty breath and the gate opened to the sound of Aunt Karen saying, "I don't see why they keep you. All you do is sit out here and hiss."

"Luce?" Dad said.

"We can talk about it later," Lucy said.

"A.K.O.S.?"

"Huh?"

"Aunt Karen Over Shoulder?" Dad chuckled again. "I'm learning Instant Messaging language."

"Oh. Well, yeah."

Aunt Karen stopped at the top of the back steps with the cooler. "Is that your father?" she said.

Lucy nodded.

"Let me talk to him when you're done."

Then that's not gonna happen, Lucy wanted to say to her. Because she never wanted to be done talking to Dad. Right now, missing him made her miss Mom even more. Mom, who would have been the coolest soccer mom ever. Who would be out there helping Mr. Auggy coach instead of telling him to smear suntan lotion all over everybody.

"Luce?" Dad said.

"Yeah, Dad," she said—barely keeping the tears out of her voice.

"We'll talk, okay? I don't want you holding things in. We agreed on that, right?"

Aunt Karen was back on the steps, arms folded, waiting.

"Right, Dad," Lucy said. "Here's Aunt Karen."

"Champ, promise me you'll hang in there."

Lucy couldn't answer. When Aunt Karen took the phone, Lucy fled with her ball to her room. She was just pulling out the Book of Lists, where she was going to write the biggest list ever to God, when she heard the ping on her window.

She stuffed the book back under her pillow and poked her head up over the windowsill. Another ping—only this time she saw the pebble as it tapped and fell. Feeling the grin creep onto her face, she searched the junkyard landscaping in front of J.J.'s house and found him there, perched on top of a stack of old tires. He let another pebble fly and missed the window. Lucy opened it.

"You wanna run?" he called to her. That was his solution to all parent problems.

"No, J.J.," she said.

"Then it's not that bad."

"Okay," she said. "It's not."

J.J. hopped down from the tire pile. "See ya," he said, and disappeared inside the dark house where she wondered if things were ever okay. Even with his mean-faced father not allowed to come around, and Winnie the nice State Lady checking in on Januarie and J.J. and their mom to make sure they had the stuff they needed, and Mr. Auggy being a substitute dad and everybody in town watching over them—even then, it wasn't an okay house.

Lucy felt a pang of guilt. At least her dad was coming home in thirty-seven more days. J.J. didn't have a dad he would ever be glad to see.

"Okay, Dad," she whispered. "I'll hang in there."

For thirty-seven more days.

4

Lucy didn't have to read the handbook Frizzy Lady talked about to know one thing about middle school: most people didn't wake up until third period.

That meant two hours without comments from the two Queen B's—who Lucy learned from Mrs. Huntington's roll call in first period were actually Bianca Aguilar and Brianna Gomez. Lucy would have bet her soccer ball they were identical twins, but according to Veronica, they weren't even related. That was amazing, because they had the same shoulder-length shiny-brown hair, identical tops that looked like girly pajamas, and they both had pink braces on their teeth. Lucy hadn't even known braces came in colors. She sure wouldn't be caught dead wearing pink ones.

They also woke up at the same time, just as the bell rang to start third period science class. Mrs. Marks droned out the roll in her boring voice, which was enough to lull Lucy into a nap, but they turned around in their seats—at exactly the same moment—and stared at her.

"What?" Lucy said.

"Why are you wearing the same shirt you wore yesterday?" Brianna said. Or was it Bianca?

"It's not the same shirt I wore yesterday," Lucy said.

"It looks the same," said Bianca. Or maybe Brianna.

"I have two of them," Lucy said.

"Why?" they said in unison.

"Because I like it." Lucy pointed to their matching green polka dot ruffly things. "Why do you two wear the same thing as each other?"

They gazed at one another as if Lucy had asked why they came to school naked.

"All right, class," Mrs. Marks said. She sounded like she was yawning. "I am going to hand out textbooks now——"

The Queen B's gave Lucy one last you-are-so-strange look and turned around. She was sure her Class Weirdo title was still in place.

Lucy was trying to pay attention to Mrs. Marks when she heard a male voice behind her say, "Hey. Half-breed."

It was a whisper, actually, but boys didn't really know how to whisper, so it came out like Mudge hissing at Aunt Karen. After checking to see that Mrs. Marks was busy with her stack of *Science For Seventh Grade*, Lucy turned around to make sure one of her cats hadn't followed her to school.

"Hey," said the boy who had grunted when 'Ricky Rodriguez' was called on the roll. He had short, messed-up-on-purpose hair and close-together eyes that were aimed at J.J. "I'm talkin' to you."

J.J. wasn't talking to *him*. In the next desk he sat with his jaw clamped down and his hands opening and closing around the end of his binder. Lucy's stomach went into a knot. That was J.J. behavior for don't-talk-to-me-or-I'll-explode.

"Hey, Sitting Bull. You no talk English?" Ricky turned and cocked a half-smile at the Queen B's, who were now watching intently. Going back to J.J., he said, "So—what about 'How'? You understand that, Half-Breed?"

Lucy folded her hands under her chin. "Do you actually live around here?" she said.

Ricky looked at Lucy for at least ten seconds before he seemed to register that she was there.

"Are you talkin' to me?" he said.

"Yeah, I'm talking to you."

"Ooh, Ricky." That came from the kid on the other side of him, the one they called Wolf-Man for some reason. He looked more like a lizard to Lucy. "She's talkin' to you, man," he said. "She likes you."

"No, actually, I don't," Lucy said. "I just want to know if he's new around here, because most people know Native Americans don't say 'how.' They probably never did."

Wolf-Man shook his lizardy little head. "She doesn't like *you*, Ricky. She likes the Half-Breed."

"It's J.J.," Lucy said, in a voice loud enough to stop Mrs. Marks two desks over. "His name is J.J."

"Leave it alone," J.J. muttered.

She did, only because his jaw muscles were twitching and Mrs. Marks was dropping the books harder on the desk tops. But as they all settled in to read the assigned introduction, "Your Exciting Year In Science," she could hear Ricky and Wolf-Man sniggering and the Queen B's whispering and her own heart pounding. Teasing her was one thing. Big deal.

But they weren't going to mess with J.J.

Dusty and Veronica were on her like two strips of Velcro as soon as they were out in the hall at the end of class.

"We have to talk," Veronica said on one side.

"Tell her, 'Ronica," Dusty said on the other.

Lucy hiked up her backpack—and noticed that both of them now had one-strap bags slung over their shoulders. "Tell me what?" she said.

Veronica pulled them around the corner, two doors down from the study hall room. "Those kids—Ricky and Wolf-Man—"

"And the two girls," Dusty said.

"The Queen B's," Lucy said.

Veronica's lower lip sagged.

"Never mind," Lucy said. "Go on—what about them?"

"They're from Coyote Hills." Veronica bounced her ponytail as if that had said it all.

"So?" Lucy said.

Dusty put her hand on Lucy's arm. "Those kids are mean—not all of them, but a lot of them. They have a really bad rep'."

Veronica tugged her other arm. "Like they can totally ruin your life if they don't like you and, Lucy, no offense, I don't think they like you."

"I don't like them either! Who cares?"

Dusty's dark eyes went wide. "We do. We don't want to see you get hurt, 'kay?"

"They can't hurt me," Lucy said. "And I'm not going to *let* them hurt J.J."

"How are you going to stop them?" Dusty said.

Lucy shrugged. "I think I already did."

Veronica's lip was now nearly to her chest. "You don't know who you're dealing with, Lucy. I think they're just getting started."

There was no 'getting started' in Frizzy Lady's study hall, however, and during lunch the Coyote Hills kids kept to their table at the other side of the cafeteria where a shooting the covers off the straws thing was going on. Fortunately, Veronica was giving the "Who's From Hotsville" report at the Dreams' table, and for once Lucy was glad, because it meant nobody talked about what had happened in third period.

J.J. said nothing at all.

"You mad at me?" Lucy said when they were messing around with the soccer ball in the courtyard later.

"No," he said.

"Ignoring them wasn't gonna work."

"I know."

"I think they're done."

J.J. didn't answer. He just looked at her like she was nuts.

But maybe she wasn't. In fifth period, most of the kids, no matter what Hills they were from, were focused on harassing Mr. Torres, who didn't seem to notice. And nobody — nobody — was going to do anything but pre-algebra in the Colonel's class. Even though Lucy got the whole idea of equations right away, she broke a sweat every time the flat-haired teacher looked her way. She would actually like to see Ricky and the Wolf-Man *try* to bully J.J. with the Colonel watching. They would probably end up getting a court martial.

So maybe middle school wasn't going to be that bad after all. Maybe all you had to do was stand up for yourself and your friends and you could go back to doing what you wanted. Lucy felt lighter that afternoon, and she even got J.J. to race bikes to the soccer field. He still wasn't talking, but he let her get almost up on his rear fender before he took off and left her at the bridge. That was a sure sign he wasn't still annoyed at her.

When they got to the field, Mr. Auggy was smiling something bigger than his usual small smile.

"It's about time, Lucy Goosey," Gabe said even before she and J.J. had dropped their bikes.

"Guess what?" Carla Rosa said. "Mr. Auggy won't tell us the good news until you and J.J. are here."

"Guess what, Carla Rosa?" Oscar said. "They're here!"

He laughed so hard at himself, he nearly lost the toothpick he was always chewing on, And when he jabbed Emanuel his pick did fall out, so he jabbed Oscar back. Mr. Auggy had to buzz them to make them stop.

"What good news?" Lucy said.

"I have a team for us to play." Mr. Auggy smiled even bigger. "It's just right up the road, but technically, you are now a traveling team."

"Road trip!" Oscar said, jabbing Emanuel yet again.

"Where are we going?" Veronica said.

"Who's this team?" Gabe said.

Mr. Auggy put his hand up. "We have a game on September twelfth. We're playing a team called the Howl. In Coyote Hills."

The air seemed to go dead until Veronica wailed, "No!"

Mr. Auggy blinked. "What's the problem?"

"She's just bein' emo, Mr. A." Gabe tugged at Veronica's ponytail, and the fear left her face like fog from a windshield.

"Seriously," Mr. Auggy said. "Is there something I should know?"

Lucy looked at J.J. He was looking back, and shaking his head so slightly she was sure nobody else could tell he was even moving.

"Nothing we can't handle, Mr. Auggy," Lucy said.

She saw Dusty lower her eyes, but J.J. let out a long breath and Carla Rosa didn't say "guess what?" because she didn't know what they were talking about and neither did Emanuel or Oscar. Gabe just shrugged, so Veronica did, too, of course.

"All right, then," Mr. Auggy said. "Let's warm up by running the gauntlet. Usual teams."

When Lucy started for her side of the field, Dusty trotted up beside her.

"Why didn't you tell Mr. Auggy?" she said. Her eyes were big pools of worry.

"Because those kids in our class from Coyote Hills probably don't even play soccer, and I doubt they're gonna come to our game."

"How do you know?"

Lucy stopped at the line and parked the ball on her hip. "Can you actually see the Queen B's going for a goal? They might break a nail."

Dusty gave a nervous giggle.

"Besides, soccer people are good people." Lucy bounced the ball lightly on top of Dusty's head. "Like us."

"You are so cool, '*lillo*," Dusty said. "I want to be like you when I grow up."

The whole practice flowed that day, like Inez's enchilada sauce over a pan of tortillas, Mr. Auggy said as he loaded Lucy's bike into the back of his Jeep to drive her home. Lucy loved to ride in his Jeep, especially when he blew the horn. It always sounded friendly, like his voice.

"I think it's because we've got something to work toward now," he said.

Lucy thought it was because Aunt Karen didn't show up with wholesome snacks and juice boxes and sunscreen.

And that, she found out when they got to her house, was because Aunt Karen had stayed home to help Inez get supper ready, since Mr. Auggy was staying. Lucy smelled Inez's enchiladas—Mr. Auggy's favorite—so she knew Aunt Karen didn't have anything to do with the food.

Her 'help' consisted of putting a table cloth on the table—where had she found that?—and setting out matching cloth napkins—okay, she'd been to Ruidoso again—and coordinating it all with a bouquet from Claudia's House of Flowers that you couldn't even see over to talk to each other.

"She put on make-up right before you got here," Mora whispered to Lucy as she was leaving with Inez. "She's totally crushing on Mr. Auggy."

That thought was so sickening Lucy was sure she wouldn't be able to eat. But the enchiladas were her favorite, too, and the conversation was all about her even-more-favorite topic: the Olympic Development Program.

At summer soccer camp, Coach Hawke had recommended Lucy to the ODP people, and they asked her to try out for the program that trained soccer players to compete for the US Olympic Soccer Team. Lucy knew, somewhere in the part of her that Mom had left behind, that she would be so proud if Lucy pursued her dream. So ever since she was invited, Lucy had a soccer ball at her feet every minute she could, but so far she didn't know what else she was supposed to do.

"I've got all the info now, Captain," Mr. Auggy said between the hunks of tortilla-wrapped chicken going into his mouth. "Here's what you're going to have to show at the try-out."

"Which is when?" Aunt Karen said, pulling her Blackberry out of her pocket. That was where she kept track of her whole life, as far as Lucy could tell. Now it looked like she was about to keep track of Lucy's there, too.

"I don't have an exact date yet," Mr. Auggy said. "Whenever it is, we need to focus on what it's going to take to make sure they know you're an elite player."

"What does 'elite' mean?" Lucy said.

"It means you're the best," Aunt Karen tapped her fingernails on the table. "So what do we do, Sam?"

We? Sam?

Lucy bulleted her eyes on Mr. Auggy and pretended Aunt Karen wasn't there.

"They're looking for four things," he said. "Skill—which is basically your ability to control the ball under game conditions—"

"Well, we *know* she can do that," Aunt Karen said.

Good grief—she was taking notes.

"Tactics—seeing opportunities, having a vision of what's happening on the field."

"Check," Aunt Karen said. Like she even knew what that meant.

"Fitness and athletic ability, and psychological attitude."

Yeah, everybody was all about Lucy's 'attitude.' She was sure it would be easier to have a good one with the ODP than it was with Aunt Karen.

"Fitness," Aunt Karen said, frowning at what she'd typed into her Blackberry. "What are we talking there, Sam?"

"You'll need to be in great shape," Mr. Auggy said, still talking directly to Lucy.

"That means good nutrition, plenty of sleep, all those things." Aunt Karen licked her lips. "All right, Sam—you take care of—" She looked at the tiny screen. "—skills, tactics, and athletic ability, and I'll work on fitness and psychological attitude."

Mr. Auggy was still looking at Lucy, and she thought she caught a tiny, tiny glimmer of irritation in his eyes.

"Actually," he said, "it's *all* going to be up to the Captain." Lucy never liked Mr. Auggy more than she did at that moment.

✳

"That's a lot to think about, Champ," Dad said on the phone later when she told him all about it.

Lucy went for the back door so she could talk in private, but Aunt Karen frowned and shook her head.

"It's too late to go outside," she said.

Lucy didn't argue with her because Dad might think that fell under 'attitude'. She wandered into the living room and curled up on what she and Dad called the Sitting Couch, because Marmalade and Artemis Hamm currently had the Napping Couch tied up.

"I'm not saying you can't do it, Champ," Dad said. "I've seen what you're capable of, you know that. But just remember—"

"I know," Lucy said, "you want me to get to be a kid. And I am."

"Just take care of what I love," he said.

Lucy promised she would, and then handed the phone to Aunt Karen who was motioning for it from the doorway.

As Lucy slid on the yellow rug to her room, she again felt light. Yes, the ODP was a big and serious deal—but that was a good thing. It would give her so much to think about that she wouldn't get all

42

tangled up in missing Dad and being the Class Weirdo and maybe even having to deal with the Coyote Hills kids a few more times before they understood that J.J. was not to be fooled with. She had to concentrate on soccer.

That was what she was doing the next morning as she deposited her soccer ball inside her new locker. Dusty and Veronica were discussing how they were going to decorate theirs—which had never occurred to Lucy—when all three of them suddenly seemed to be surrounded.

The Queen B's, dressed in stripes that ran together and made them look like they were both in the same hoodie, were flanked by two bigger girls Lucy recognized from their class. They sat in the back every period, thumbs racing across their phones, except in sixth because of the Colonel.

"This is her," Bianca/Brianna said. One of them pointed at Lucy.

"You're not serious," the taller girl said. She had very long, very curly, very yellow hair and a thin nose that seemed to go from her forehead all the way down to her chin. In fact, everything about her was long, including the way she dragged out her words. "You are *not* serious," she said again.

"You're on the Los Suenos Dreams?" the other one said. It was as if she were the exact opposite of her friend in every way—boy-short dark hair, a wide face, and a quick way of talking that made her spit when she spoke.

One of the Queen B's pointed at Lucy's shirt, and then looked disappointed.

"Okay, she's not wearing it today, but all the other days we've been at school she's worn that t-shirt that says it right on it."

"I'm on the Dreams," Lucy said. "So?"

"Me, too," Dusty piped up. She gave Veronica a long look until Veronica nodded like she was admitting to robbing a convenience store.

The tall girl folded her arms. "You are so dead," she said.

"Yeah, we are going to slaughter you," the short version said. A speck of saliva flew into the air.

Brianna pulled her slick lips into a smug smile. "We're on the Coyote Hills Howl."

Lucy felt her eyes pop open.

Tall Girl pulled her long gaze up and down Lucy.

Was that supposed to make her shrivel up or something? That seemed to be what Tall Girl expected, but Lucy almost laughed. It was time to cut this whole thing off at the knees.

"Oh," she said. "Then we're going to be worthy opponents. I'm Lucy. This is Dusty and Veronica. Who are you?"

Brianna pointed to Long Girl. "This is Skye," she said, as if Lucy had asked the President who he was. "And Nina. Everybody knows them."

"I didn't," Lucy said, "so I guess everybody doesn't."

Bianca shook her head. "You just get weirder all the time."

"What did you call us?" Skye said. Her eyes narrowed close to the long nose so that she was beginning to look cross-eyed to Lucy.

"Worthy opponents," Dusty said, too cheerily. "Don't you love that?"

Nina pulled her chin in so far it almost disappeared into her neck. "You're not our 'worthy opponents,'" she said, spitting within inches of Lucy's nose. "We are gonna take you before the half. You'll never score against us."

Until that point, Veronica hadn't said a word. But she piped up now with, "Is it an all-girl team?"

"Do you, like, live in a cave or something?" Brianna said.

"Hello," Bianca said. "Ricky. Wolf-Man."

"Oh!" Veronica said.

Lucy jabbed her before she could say, "They're hot!"

"Plus four eighth graders you probably don't know," Bianca said.

"Since you don't know anybody," Brianna said.

Lucy didn't say anything this time.

"Well?" Skye said.

"Well, what?"

Skye hissed. She actually hissed. The whole team was starting to sound like a litter of kittens.

"Come on," Skye said, and she led her parade down the hall. Lucy had the urge to laugh again.

"I don't think this is going to be that much fun," Dusty said when they were gone.

"Ya think?" Veronica said.

They both looked at Lucy.

"Playing against two Queen B's, a Spitter, and a Hisser?" Lucy said. "It doesn't get any more fun than that."

"Really?" Veronica said, lip hanging.

"So you don't think they're really going to slaughter us, *Bolillo*?" Dusty said.

"We're not pigs," Lucy said. "It's a soccer game, not a barbecue."

Veronica gave a nervous giggle. Dusty lifted the chin, the pointy part of her heart-shaped face. "Okay, if you can stand up to them, so can we."

"Nothing to stand up to," Lucy said. "It's all show with them. But us—we're the real thing."

She hoped that was what an elite player would say.

5

When Lucy got home that afternoon, Mora leaped up from the kitchen table, freaking Marmalade out of his chair and sending him flying into the living room in an orange blur. Lucy bet he was headed straight under the Napping Couch. Mora's hands had so many punctuation marks going, Lucy felt like she was in Mrs. Huntington's class.

"Okay—I tried to tell her, Lucy—but she just doesn't get that we are in middle school now and we don't need Bible study. Hello! Not little girls any more!"

"Mora," Inez said from the sink. "Sit."

"You try talking to her," Mora said to Lucy as she flounced herself back to her chair. "She'll probably listen to you—I mean, who am I? Just her granddaughter!"

She slashed out a final exclamation point with her finger and fell into the seat. "Well?" she said.

"Well—" Lucy parked her backpack next to the hall doorway and watched Inez's back. For a short lady, she could stand tall when she meant business. She was about six foot four right now. "It depends on what we're going to study."

Mora sat straight up. "Whose side are you on?"

"There is no side," Inez said. She set a small bowl of melted cheese on the table, the smell of which pulled Lucy to her chair like a magnet. Anything was worth Inez's *queso* and tortillas.

"I think that means we're doing it, Mora," Lucy said.

Inez turned back to the counter, and Mora's eyes rolled all the way up into her head.

"You're a traitor," she whispered to Lucy.

"No." Lucy nodded at Inez's back. "I'm a coward."

You didn't question Inez when she stood like a mountain. And besides, Inez's weekly Bible study had actually helped her in the past. She wouldn't know half of what she did understand about how to be a girl—since her mom wasn't there—if it weren't for Ruth and Rachel and Leah and Esther—the Old Testament women. None of them played soccer, but she was pretty sure they would have if the game had been around back then.

"All right," Mora said with a deeper-than-necessary sigh. "What's her name?"

Inez set the shallow dish of tortillas next to the queso and lifted the lid for them. Steam wafted out.

"*Senorita* Maria," she said.

"That would be Mary," Mora said to Lucy. "Now, her I've heard of. I played her in a Christmas play one time."

Lucy dunked a piece of tortilla into the melted cheese. The only time she'd been in a Christmas play was when she was four, when they lived in Albuquerque. The Sunday school teacher made her play an angel, even though she wanted to be a sheep. She'd tried out the wings during the performance and fallen off the back of the platform. They wouldn't let her be in it at all the next year.

Inez opened her Bible with its cracked leather cover and smoothed her hands over the pages. Lucy was always surprised they didn't tear because they were like the very thinnest part of an onion's skin. But, then, Inez always handled her Bible as if it were a newborn kitten. She even spoke its stories that way.

"Senorita Mary," she began. "Her story is told by *Senor* Luke." She ran a tender finger beside the verses. "She is a young girl, maybe only some older than you. She is engage to Senor Joseph."

Lucy hid a smile. She like the way Inez talked, as if she were still just learning English. But she didn't want Inez to think she was laughing at her. Mora did enough of that.

"She is alone one day when the angel, Senor Gabriel, he comes to visit her in her town of Nazareth."

"Wait a minute," Mora said. "I already know this story. He tells her she's going to have a baby and she does and that's where we get Christmas."

Even Lucy knew there was more to it than that.

"Listen, Mora," Inez said.

Mora shrugged and twirled a string of cheese around her finger.

"Senor Angel Gabriel he says to Maria that she is highly favored and the Lord is with her, and she is *muy temeroso*."

"That means this was freaking her out," Mora said.

"Senor Angel Gabriel, he says to her that God has chosen her to give the birth to a son name Jesus and he will be the Son of God."

Mora licked her fingers. "Like I said—she had the baby and we get presents."

"You are Mary," Inez said.

"Excuse me?" Mora said.

"You want us to pretend we're Mary," Lucy said.

"*Si.*"

"So—an angel has just come to tell me I'm going to have a baby," Lucy said.

"*Si.*"

"Well, first of all, I'm not even married," Mora said.

"*Si.*"

Mora's already huge brown eyes swelled. "Not good." She turned to Lucy. "You're supposed to have a husband before you have a baby, because—"

"I *know*," Lucy said. Just because she didn't keep a record of which boys were "hot" didn't mean she didn't know about that kind of stuff.

"Not only a *bebé*," Inez said. "But the baby of God. Think of Mary telling this to others."

"Who would believe her?" Lucy said.

"*Si.* And she can be in big trouble for having the baby with no husband."

"Let me get this straight," Mora said. "It was supposed to be this huge honor, like God was doing her a favor. Only she could get in major trouble for it?"

"She can be thrown from the town. Maybe killed."

"Nuh-uh!" Lucy said.

Mora shook her head "I would have been so out of there."

"But Senorita Mary, no. She say to the angel—" Inez turned to the page, "'May it be to me as you have said.'"

"And we're supposed to think like her?" Mora said. "It's a good thing God didn't ask me to do that."

Lucy had to agree with her there.

"The Senor Angel Gabriel tells her another thing."

"How to make her parents believe her, I hope!" Mora said. Her fingers were stabbing exclamation points into the air again.

"No. He say her cousin, Senora Elizabeth, will have a baby also."

"At least she had a husband," Mora said. She looked at Lucy. "You can tell that because she's a senora, not a senorita."

"Hello, I'm not a moron," Lucy said.

"Senora Elizabeth, she is very old," Inez said.

Mora frowned. "I thought you said she was pregnant. "

"Sí. The angel, he tells Senorita Mary, 'Nothing is impossible with God.'"

"Evidently not," Mora said.

Lucy got up on one knee. She was pretty sure they hadn't done this part of the story in the Christmas play. "So what does Elizabeth have to do with it?" she said.

"Senorita Mary, she goes to Judea to visit Senora Elizabeth—"

"Like for a baby shower or something," Mora put in.

"And when the Senora sees her young cousin, the baby inside her, he leaps for the joy."

Lucy thought that would be an incredibly weird feeling, but she nodded for Inez to go on.

"The Senora, she says Senorita Mary is blessed because she believe what the Lord has say to her."

"Even though everybody is going to think Mary is making the whole thing up," Lucy said.

Inez never smiled all the way, but she looked pleased now. "Sí," she said, "and Senorita Mary, she is so fill with God, she sings a beautiful song."

Mora put her hand up like a stop sign. "You're not going to sing it, are you, Abuela? I mean, we're not in a musical here."

Lucy kind of wished Inez would. But Inez merely closed her eyes and said, "The Senorita, she sing that she is the most blessed girl in the world and that this God-Son she will have will take care of the poor and save his children, like he have promised."

"How did she get that out of Elizabeth's kid doing a dance in her stomach?" Mora said.

"She knows the history of her family," Inez said. "How *El Senor* has been working and speaking among his people for two thousand years. She knows how he turn things around."

Lucy got up on her other knee. "Turns them around—what does that mean?"

"He takes down the people who think they are high and mighty and shows them who is in charge." Inez's eyes glowed. "He puts down the people at the top and lift up the people at the bottom."

Lucy sank, disappointed, back on her heels. "No offense, Inez, but I don't think that happened." If it had, there would be no Queen B's and Coyote Hills kids and wars in Iraq and moms who didn't come home from them.

Inez was watching her. "It is happening still, Senorita Lucy," she said. "Senor God, he is not finish. He will work in each life."

"Uh, no thanks," Mora said. "I don't want a baby right now."

Inez ignored her. "When you pray with your lists, Senorita Lucy, you ask God to speak. He will speak of this and you will obey. Or not."

"Lucy—shouldn't you be at soccer practice?"

Aunt Karen's voice was so wrong right then, Lucy whipped around in her chair to be sure she hadn't imagined it. But her aunt was there, a phone thing in her ear—Lucy thought Mora had called it a Blue Tooth—and an odd pair of glasses with only half their lenses perched on the end of her nose. She looked at the watch that dangled like a bracelet on her wrist and licked her lips.

"What about practice?" she said again—this time to Inez.

"This is Bible study day," Lucy said. "I go to practice after. Mr. Auggy knows—"

"Does that give you enough time, though?" Aunt Karen pulled off the glasses and stuck them on top of her head. "I'd better drive you, then." Again she looked at the watch. "I have a conference call with some clients in ten minutes, but—"

"I'll go on my bike," Lucy said. "Can I go get my stuff, Inez?"

Inez just nodded and kept her eyes away from Aunt Karen. Lucy was in her room stuffing her cleats into her backpack when Aunt Karen came in without knocking. Lollipop dove into the toy chest.

"Was that the fat black one?" Aunt Karen said.

"Lollipop," Lily said, and gave her cleats a too-hard shove into the pack.

"I keep finding her in my room. I think she took one of my gold hoop earrings."

"She doesn't even have pierced ears," Lucy said.

"Cute."

Aunt Karen closed the door and glanced over her shoulder like somebody might be listening outside. Lucy didn't point out that *she* was the only one in the house who ever invaded anybody else's privacy.

"I think we need to rethink your schedule," Aunt Karen said. "Bible study's nice and I know your father wants you to have it, but if it's cutting into your soccer time—"

"This is the way I always do it," Lucy said.

"But you haven't 'always' been preparing for a tryout that could totally change your life. You have to stay focused."

Lucy yanked the zipper closed and flung her backpack over her shoulder and went over the no eye-rolling-door-slamming-heavy-sighing rules in her head. All she could do was hold her breath.

"Well, don't be any later for practice," Aunt Karen said. "I'll come up with a tentative schedule for you and we'll talk later, all right?"

Lucy grunted. At least the rules didn't say she couldn't do that.

When she opened the back door, the shadow from the Mexican elder tree was already spidering across the patio. There really wouldn't be much time to practice before dark. She was about to close the door behind her and hurry down the steps when she heard Aunt Karen say, "There's no need for you to cook now that I'm here."

Lucy froze, hand on the doorknob.

"Senor Ted, he hired me to make the suppers." Inez's voice was low.

"That's because all he can do is nuke frozen dinners. Now that I'm here, there isn't any reason for you to continue to fix dinner."

Except that Inez was the best cook ever and Aunt Karen—Lucy didn't think she'd ever eaten anything Aunt Karen fixed. All she knew how to make was reservations at a restaurant.

"Senor Ted, he is not please with the food?"

Hello! Dad loved her food!

"That isn't the point." Even through the crack in the door Lucy heard Aunt Karen sigh. "Look, I know the way you cook is a cultural thing, and I love a killer enchilada myself now and then—but all this starch and fat isn't good for Lucy, especially not with her being in training. She needs—"

Lucy flung the door open. "I need chili *rellenos* and *sopapillas!*"

"Why are you not on your way to the soccer field?"

"Because I—"

"You don't have a dog in this fight, Lucy," Aunt Karen said.

"What dog?" Mora said from the table.

Inez hissed at her. Lucy barely kept from hissing herself.

Aunt Karen stood with her arms folded and her eyebrows up to her hairline. "You heard what Mr. Auggy said. You have to be in top physical shape for the tryouts, and that isn't going to happen eating like this."

She shot a hand over the queso bowl. Mora peered into it suspiciously.

"Did you ask Dad about it?" Lucy said.

"Senorita Lucy."

Lucy looked at Inez. Her face had no expression, except for the sparks in her eyes.

"Go," she said.

Lucy didn't argue. Even Mora didn't question Inez when she looked like that. As Lucy took the back steps down two at a time, she was just glad she wasn't Aunt Karen right now.

Everybody was already warming up when Lucy got to the soccer field, and Mr. Auggy started the day's drill as soon as she arrived.

"Monkey in the Middle!" he said.

"Guess what?" Carla Rosa said. "I don't remember what that is."

Gabe snorted. "Big surprise."

Mr. Auggy gave him a buzz. "How about you remind Carla Rosa about Monkey in the Middle — using your best good-sport attitude, naturally."

Lucy wanted to say she didn't think Gabe *had* a good-sport attitude, but she didn't want to get buzzed, too.

"Okay, C.R.," Gabe said, beefy hands on his hips like super-jock, "it's the one where you get in threes, and two of you team up and try to keep possession of the ball while you're passing it back and forth and the one in the middle tries to get it away from you." He wiggled his eyebrows. "Which — good luck if you get between me and the J-Man, 'cause it ain't gonna happen."

"Guess what, Gabe?" Mr. Auggy said before Carla Rosa could. "I'm putting Lucy between you and J.J."

Lucy liked to think Gabe looked the tiniest bit scared before he grinned in that chimpanzee way he had and said, "Bring her on."

Although Lucy would rather have been with *Dusty* and J.J., she had to admit doing any drill with Gabe made her play harder and better.

"You're working your way away from your own goal, end people," Mr. Auggy called out. "Middle players, work your way toward it and try to score."

"Like I said, good luck." Gabe parted his lips, ape-like, at J.J. and lofted the ball over Lucy's head. It headed for the ground in front of J.J., who held his foot out and up in the air so the ball would land on it. Lucy charged for the ball and J.J. lost his balance. She captured it and made what Mr. Auggy called a mad-dog dribble in the other direction, laughing into the air.

"You won't be laughin' for long, Lucy Goosey!" Gabe called to her.

She could hear both of them behind her, and she recognized J.J.'s breathing first as he came alongside and easily made the tackle that snatched the ball in mid-dribble. He was headed back toward her goal almost before she realized he had it. She could see his shoulders shaking with silent laughter. She hardly ever actually heard him laugh. She just sort of felt it.

Which meant now might be a good time to bring up a topic she'd been avoiding all day.

As J.J. and Gabe lazily passed the ball back and forth, almost waiting for Lucy to catch up, she trotted toward them and said, "Hey, J.J. — you know Wolf-Man and that Ricky kid are on the Howl, right?"

J.J. smacked the ball a little harder than he had to and it booted down the field. Lucy raced Gabe for it and got there first. As she turned to reposition the ball, she saw that J.J. wasn't laughing any more.

"You didn't know," she said.

"So what?" Gabe said.

He was low, legs apart, knees bent, arms out, but although his eyes were on the ball, Lucy figured she had his mind on what she was saying. She faked to one side and then the other, and Gabe fell for it. She took off again with both of them on her heels.

"Are you okay with that, J.J.?" she said over her shoulder.

"With what?" he said.

"With playing those guys? I know they treat you bad — "

"Would you shut up and pay attention, Lucy Goosey?" Gabe said. He was trying to block her vision, just like Mr. Auggy had taught them.

"They're all show, J.J.," Lucy said as she tried not to let Gabe slow her down. "They can't hurt you on the field or — "

The rest of the words tripped over themselves as Gabe cut between her and the goal and tried to push her to the side with his big-time defending. At least, that was what he was supposed to do. But suddenly his big chest was in her face and she couldn't help plowing into him. Before she could get her arms up they were both on the ground, Gabe halfway on top of her, laughing like a hyena.

"Get off me!" she said, trying not to laugh herself. "Foul, Mr. Auggy! Gabe, I said get off me!"

"Hello-o!"

Lucy rolled over and looked up at Veronica, who was standing over them, lower lip hanging, upper lip curled, if that was even possible.

"Get him off me, Veronica," Lucy said.

She expected Veronica to peel Gabe up with her long, skinny arms and pat him down for bruises. But she took a step back and folded those arms across her chest.

"He can just get up his own self," she said. She flipped her ponytail around. "J.J.—do you want a new partner?"

Her voice went up into the place she reserved for Gabe—or whoever else she deemed "hot" at the moment. Lucy felt her own mouth fall open. Was Veronica actually doing the boy-crazy thing with *J.J.?*

If she was, J.J. didn't appear to have a clue. He got the ball into place with his foot and dribbled off to the other end of the field, leaving Gabe and Lucy still on the ground.

"Are you *serious?*" Veronica said to Lucy.

"About what?" Lucy said.

Veronica's eyes rolled up into her brain, as far as Lucy could tell, and she huffed off. Lucy twisted around to find J.J., who was juggling the ball way down the field, but not so far that Lucy couldn't see his jaw muscles twitching. *What* was going on?

Gabe snickered and got to his feet and stuck his hand down to Lucy.

"What?" she said.

"I'll help you up," he said.

"Are you nuts?" Lucy smacked his hand away and stood up by herself. She started to head for J.J., but Mr. Auggy blew his whistle and called for a different drill—one where J.J. avoided her and Veronica shot her girl-drama looks and Gabe took every chance to nudge Lucy and poke her and get in her space when she was trying to get the ball down the field. And when Mr. Auggy finally announced practice was over, J.J. took off on his bike like he had a whole pack of mad dogs after him. Lucy had to take off, too, to get away from Gabe and get home to talk to Mora. For once, she wanted her advice about boys—like how to get one off who suddenly decided she was the other half of his Velcro.

But when she got to her house, just as the elder tree shadows and the twilight were blending into one big gray mass, Inez's truck was gone. And there was no smell of melted cheese and cilantro. Aunt Karen was at the sink, washing lettuce.

"How was practice?" she said.

"Fine," Lucy said. "What are you doing?"

"Making a salad. Dinner's almost ready."

"I'm not hungry."

"I want you to drink the protein shake in the refrigerator."

Lucy didn't even answer. And she didn't ride the Navajo rug as she charged to her room. She pulled out her Book of Lists and her pen and wrote savagely—

DEAR GOD: WHY I CAN'T BE LIKE MARY EVEN THOUGH INEZ SAYS TO THINK LIKE I'M HER.

1. I can't say 'let it be for me like you said' — or however that goes because I don't think YOU said Aunt Karen could take over my whole entire life. My schedule. My FOOD!

2. It doesn't seem like you're taking care of your children like Mary said in that song. What about Inez? She practically knows the Bible by heart, but Aunt Karen gets away with acting like she's trying to poison me.

3. You're supposed to be knocking down the people at the top and lifting up the people at the bottom, so what about Aunt Karen? She's at the top of everything right now and I don't know if I can wait around for you to knock her off.

4. And how come you made boys so complicated? Just talking to them is like figuring out an algebra problem. Why did Mary even WANT a husband?

Lollipop meowed from inside the toy chest. Lucy put the Book of Lists back under the pillow and poked her head into the chest. Yellow eyes blinked at her. Everything else was black, except for a shiny flash by her tail.

Lolli gave another protest cry as Lucy pulled it out. She felt her grin spread when she saw that it was Aunt Karen's gold hoop earring.

"You're safe, Lolli," Lucy said, scooping her black roundness out of the chest. "I'm not gonna tell on you."

Lollipop didn't look convinced as she hid her face in the crook of Lucy's arm.

"Seriously. I'll protect you from her." Lucy buried her own face in black fur and whispered, "I just want somebody to do that for me, and it's not happening."

Lolli burrowed in further, and Lucy remembered something. Something Inez said.

It is happening still, Senorita Lucy. Ask God to speak. You will obey.

Lucy tucked Lolli onto the windowsill and pulled out the book again and tapped her pen on a new page.

"Okay," she said. "I'll ask. But just remember: I'm no Mary."

And then she wrote until the page was filled.

6

God didn't send an angel to tell Lucy the answers to all the questions she wrote in her book Thursday night.

Not that she was really expecting Gabriel to show up in her room, though it would have been nice. The first person she saw when she went out of her gate Friday morning was Gabe—which *was* short for Gabriel, but she was pretty sure that didn't count. He didn't even come close to being an angel.

"Lucy Goosey," he said.

"What?" She looked past him to see if J.J. was coming, but there was no sign of him yet. "Where is everybody?"

"Who needs everybody when you got me?"

Lucy grunted. "Like I said, where is everybody?"

"Dude, that's harsh." Gabe shrugged his big shoulders, and then he just stood there looking at her. At least he didn't get all close to her like he did during soccer practice, but still he was acting very weird, even for Gabe.

"*What?*" Lucy said.

"If I say something are you gonna go all emo?"

"What *is* 'emo' anyway?" Lucy put up her hand. "Never mind. I don't want to know."

Gabe answered her anyway. "It's like when girls get all emotional and start yelling and crying and stuff."

"Like Veronica."

"Yeah."

"Then, no, I'm not gonna go 'emo.' Just say it."

"Okay. Stop acting big and bad around the Coyote Hills kids."

Lucy felt her eyes bulge. "Are you serious?"

Gabe raised his hand like he was about to take the witness stand. "No joke, you gotta back off."

"You don't back off!"

"I don't have to."

"Why?" Lucy said. "Because you're a boy?"

The hair on the back of her neck was standing up the way Mudge's did when he was about to climb up someone's leg. She looked again for J.J., but he still wasn't coming.

"No," Gabe said. "Because I don't get all up in their dental work to begin with."

"What dental work? What are you *talking* about, Gabe?"

"Don't you ever watch TV or anything? It just means *you* get all freaked out every time they smart off, and *I* don't."

Lucy finally heard the creak of J.J.'s front door. She tried to move past Gabe, but he stepped in her way, just like he had during Monkey in the Middle. Only there was no ball to go after.

"Why do you all of a sudden care about what I say to other people?" Lucy said.

"Because if you don't knock it off, they're gonna make trouble."

Lucy squinted up at him. "How do you know that?"

"I heard stuff. In the boys' bathroom when they were—"

"Hello! I don't want to hear about what goes on in your restroom! Just skip to what they said—no, wait. J.J.'s coming. He should hear, too."

Gabe's eyes flickered. "He's coming?"

"Yeah."

"Then just listen." His already low voice dipped downward, so that Lucy had to lean in to hear him, icky as that was. "It sounds like they're out to get the J-Man, just because he's Indian," Gabe said. "Like, from the reservation, not the country India—"

"I *know*, Gabe—"

"—and because he won't stand up for himself."

"He can't," Lucy said between her teeth. "That Winnie lady from the

State will put him in foster care if he gets in trouble for fighting. They'll say he's like his dad." She glanced nervously through the opening Gabe made with his bent elbow. J.J. was getting closer. "We have to protect him," she whispered.

"Okay, so, what is going on?" said a voice behind Lucy.

It was Veronica, sounding like she'd just walked in on a robbery in progress. Gabe wiggled his eyebrows.

"I was just having a private conversation with Lucy Goosey."

"Ooh—look out, J-Man," said still another voice—Oscar's. "Gabe's tryin' to steal your girlfriend."

"Stop it," Dusty said. "You know 'lillo and J. aren't dating—"

Where did everybody come from all of a sudden? The one time Lucy wanted to talk to Gabe alone and there they all were.

"Come on," Dusty said. "We're going to be late."

Everyone else followed her across the street, but Veronica latched onto Lucy's backpack strap and held her in place.

"Do you like Gabe now?" she said into Lucy's ear.

"Are you nuts?!"

"Well, you were all close to him—"

"We were talking in private!"

"Were you talking 'in private' all through soccer practice yesterday, too?"

"We weren't even talking yesterday!"

"Then what about today? What were you talking about just now?"

"About—"

Veronica waited, lip sagging. "About me?"

Lucy swallowed. "No," she said.

"Then what?"

"I can't tell you yet."

Veronica let go of Lucy's strap, and her eyes went into slits. "You do like him. You asked him out and you're waiting to see if he says yes."

"You are nuts," Lucy said.

Veronica shook her head, ponytail jittering, and backed away. "No, I know when somebody's trying to steal my boyfriend. I totally thought we were friends."

To Lucy's horror, Veronica's face contorted as if she were either going to throw up or cry. This had to be the 'emo' Gabe was talking about.

"I don't want your boyfriend," Lucy said.

"But I think he wants you. And I'm going to find out."

She took off after Gabe, who was sauntering ahead of them, and Lucy let her go. Why would anybody even want a boyfriend if this was what happened? Once again, in her opinion, Mary should have stuck to being without a husband.

It was even more apparent as the morning passed that no angels were going to show up with answers like they did for Mary.

Mrs. Huntington made them do a writing sample in first period, a paragraph about their first week of middle school. Lucy was still trying to turn her list of things she could actually talk about into sentences, the way Mr. Auggy had taught them, when the bell rang. She expected to be put back in the slow class before the day was over.

In social studies, Mr. Lopez made then read out loud. Lucy managed to be in the restroom when it was her turn. In science, Mrs. Marks showed a movie about amoebas, which gave everybody a chance to get caught up on their correspondence. Lucy got a note from the Queen B's saying they were glad she'd worn a different shirt but this was still her second Class Weirdo warning, one from Dusty asking if she did like Gabe but she just didn't want to hurt Veronica's feelings, and one from an anonymous sender who said, "Don't count on scoring any goals." Like that one was hard to figure out.

Lucy dumped all the notes in the trash can between classes, but there was a fresh one waiting for her when she sat down at her table in study hall.

Captain,

It said,

Will you meet me at the front of the school at the end of the day?

It was signed:

Mr. Auggy.

Was this for real? Lucy looked around, but nobody was looking sly, and it *was* in his handwriting. But how had he gotten it here?

62

Okay, so maybe there *were* angels. She just hoped the message was a good one, because this day was really getting on her last nerve. Ms. Pasqual, Frizzy Lady, was having a particularly bad hair day and barked every time anybody breathed.

That wouldn't be so bad if she weren't letting the Coyote Kids practically have a board meeting in the back of the room when they all went at the same time to sharpen the pencils they weren't using. Lucy tried not to think about what Gabe said, but it was hard when she was sure they were planning their next attack on J.J.

Lucy put her own pencil to paper to add to last night's list in the Book later:

1. It isn't just Aunt Karen that needs to be knocked down from the top. What about the CHKs?

2. J.J. needs to be lifted up from the bottom.

She closed her eyes and prayed that God would hurry up with that.

"Are you sleeping in my class, Rooney?"

Lucy's eyes sprang open. Frizzy Lady was, as Gabe would say, up in her dental work.

"No," Lucy said.

"You had your eyes closed."

"I wasn't sleeping," Lucy said.

"What were you doing then, checking your eyelids for light leaks?"

The class groaned more than laughed, but it was still enough for Lucy to want to roll her eyes. She decided right then that it was good Dad had given her the list of bad attitude behaviors or she would probably be on her way to the discipline office by now. The ODP probably wouldn't like that, either.

"Come on, Rooney, I'm waiting for an answer."

"I was praying," Lucy said.

That got a laugh. This time Ms. Pasqual barked it to silence and jabbed her finger toward the door.

"Out in the hall, Rooney," she said. "Let's go."

The only sound at that point was Dusty gasping—until the door was closed behind them. Then the whole classroom turned into a bee farm. Ms. Pasqual let it go as she crossed her arms over her very-large chest. Lucy's stomach went into a square knot.

"The law says I can't talk about my faith in the classroom," Frizzy Lady spat out at her. "But I will not allow a student to belittle it."

"I don't think I—"

"Prayer is not a joke to me."

"It isn't to me—"

"You don't have to believe what I believe, but you do have to respect it. Are we clear?"

Lucy waited to make sure that was really a question she was supposed to answer.

"Are you a mute, girl? I said 'are we clear?'"

"*I* am," Lucy said. "But *you* probably aren't because you haven't let me say anything."

Ms. Pasqual's hair seemed to frizz right up her head, and Lucy held her breath. She hadn't meant to say it exactly like that, but with Frizzy Lady pinching squeezing off her every word, she had to get it out somehow. The choice now was between mumbling she was sorry and hoping she didn't get suspended for life, or standing up for herself and *definitely* getting suspended for life.

She decided and let out the air. "I was trying to say that I really was praying," Lucy said, "and I take it way serious. And if you believe in God and Jesus and the Bible then we believe the same because I do, too." Lucy checked for tone, but she was pretty sure she was still okay. Just in case, though, she ended with, "I'm not sure what 'belittle' means, but I don't think I was doing that. Not on purpose."

Ms. Pasqual still had her arms so tightly crossed, Lucy was sure they were stopping her heartbeat. But at least she wasn't dragging her to the office. Yet.

"All right," Ms., Pasqual said after the longest pause in school history. "We'll see. Go on back in."

Lucy wasn't sure what it was they were going to 'see,' but since it wasn't going to happen that minute, she hurried back to her table. Between Dusty's bug-eyed looks and Veronica's almost-tears and J.J.'s slide down into his seat—not to mention the smothered snickers from the Coyote Kids—it was the end of the period before Lucy realized her list was gone.

As the class filed out of the study hall, most of them lifting their lips in her direction, Lucy dumped her backpack on the table and rummaged through every notebook and uncrumpled every wad of paper, but they were all just the false starts of her paragraph from first period. The list wasn't there.

"*'Lillo?'*" Dusty said from the doorway, "Are you okay?"

"I lost something," Lucy said.

She stuffed everything back into her backpack and flung it over her shoulder. Its contents went flying like big pieces of confetti. She'd forgotten to zip it.

"You aren't okay."

Dusty hurried across the room and crouched down to retrieve a handful of papers.

"You always hide it when you're upset," she said, "but I know. Ms. Pasqual was so mean to you, I'd have been, like, hysterical if it were me. Oh—" She stopped and held up the note from Mr. Auggy. "You got one of these, too."

"Did you?" Lucy said.

Dusty nodded and lowered her voice, even though there was nobody else in the room. "'Ronica didn't, though, I don't think, so don't say anything to her."

"She's not speaking to me anyway," Lucy said. "She thinks I'm trying to steal Gabe from her. Ew."

Dusty stuck Lucy's science book into the pack and soundly zipped it up. "She's probably way too sorry for you right now to be mad at you."

"She doesn't need to feel sorry for me," Lucy said as they wove among the tables for the door. "I didn't get in trouble." She gave the room one last look. "I just lost a piece of paper I was writing on."

"Oh, no! Was it your math homework?"

Lucy shook her head. Okay, so it wasn't *that* big a disaster.

"Frizzy Lady probably threw it away or something," Lucy said.

Dusty giggled and looped her arm through Lucy's. "Frizzy Lady? You're so funny, *'lillo*."

Lucy laughed a little, too, and felt better and hoped the juice hadn't sogged up the bread on the peanut butter and pickle sandwich she'd made for herself before Aunt Karen stumbled out into the kitchen.

"My lunch is in my locker," she said to Dusty. "I'll catch up."

Maybe there weren't angels, she decided as she made her way down the vacant hall. But there were some good things, which meant maybe God was speaking, in a weird sort of way. Only two and a half more hours before she and Dusty would find out what Mr. Auggy had in store. Life might be good again.

Until she turned the corner to her locker and ran straight into Skye. And Nina.

"We got a question for you," Nina said, spitting *directly* into Lucy's dental work.

"Are we the CHKs?" Skye said.

And then she dangled the list before Lucy's eyes.

7

Lucy reached out to snatch the list, but Nina caught her by the wrist and squeezed.

"What is this? WWE?" Lucy said.

She used her soccer-built muscles to wrench her arm away. With the other one, she grabbed her paper out of Skye's surprised hand and crammed it into the pocket of her sweatshirt. She really wanted to shove it right up Nina's nose, but Dad would definitely not like that. Neither would the ODP. She was *very* sure that wouldn't be a good psychological attitude.

Nina took a step toward Lucy, breathing like a bus, but Skye put out a long, freckled arm to stop her. Her face lengthened another two inches, Lucy was certain.

"So, what do you do?" Skye said, pulling out her words like they were on a string. "Go around knocking people down?"

"Huh?" Lucy said, although she knew what they were talking out. *It isn't just Aunt Karen that needs to be knocked down from the top,* she had written. She almost laughed.

"What's so funny?" Nina said. She pressed against Skye's arm like she was trying to push a gate open.

"*I* don't knock anybody down."

"Then who's Aunt Karen?" Skye said.

"Forget that," Nina said. "Are we the CHKs? Coyote Hills—" She held up both palms, face twisted into a question mark. "Klutzes? Kriminals?"

"Or do you just not know how to spell 'chicks'?" Skye said.

"I know how to spell 'chicks,'" Lucy said. "I also know how to spell 'criminals'—and it isn't with a 'k'."

"Look, are we the CHKs or not?" Skye said, "Because if we are, you just better know—"

"—You will not be knocking us down."

Lucy didn't point out to Nina that the list didn't say *she* was going to knock anybody down. If *Ms. Pasqual* had almost flipped out when she mentioned God, there was no telling what these two would do. Besides, she wanted to end this conversation before they started in on the second item on her list.

She hitched up her backpack and turned toward her locker. That sandwich was definitely going to be soggy by now.

Skye followed her and said, "Oh, and just so you know."

"Uh-huh." Lucy twirled her combination.

"We showed your note to Ricky. He said to tell you that J.J. kid—"

Lucy stopped her lock on the '5'.

"He's never gonna be anywhere *but* the bottom. Especially after today."

Skye turned on her heel and walked toward Nina at the end of the row of lockers. Lucy listened to the squeaks of her tennis shoes and to the warnings in her head.

No attitude. Back off. Just ignore them.

But this was J.J.

"Well, I guess Ricky would know," Lucy said.

The two girls whirled around.

"How?" Skye said.

"Because—he's right there at the bottom, lookin' up."

"Do you girls not know this area is off limits during lunch?"

Lucy went automatically to attention at the sound of the Colonel's voice. Skye and Nina looked like they were about to salute as he marched toward them.

"We were just telling her that," Skye said.

Nina bobbed her head.

"I didn't realize you were hall monitors." The Colonel looked at them for so long Lucy thought they were going to evaporate. "You have ten seconds to get to the cafeteria," he said.

Skye and Nina did a double-time, stiff-legged walk down the hall. Lucy grabbed her now sodden lunch bag out of her locker and slammed the door shut. When she turned, the Colonel was still standing there.

"Don't get yourself in trouble your first week," he said.

You have no idea, she wanted to tell him. Instead, she just said, "Yes, sir," and started to flee.

"Did I say you could go?"

Lucy skidded to a stop. God could send an angel any minute now and that would be just fine.

"Sorry," she said as she turned back to him.

His face had lost some of its stiffness, and he was rubbing his chin with his hand. "Are you any relation to Ted Rooney?" he said. "NPR?"

"Yes, sir," Lucy said.

The Colonel stared at her, hard, and Lucy didn't know what she was supposed to say. She chose nothing.

"He's a good man," the Colonel said finally. "I miss him on the radio."

"He'll be back," Lucy said.

"I hope so. Meanwhile, you make him proud." He shot a look down the hall where the CHKs had disappeared. "Just stay out of trouble."

Lucy wasn't sure whether he was talking to them or her, and she decided not to ask.

By then there was no time to eat and her sandwich had turned to soup anyway, so she went straight to the courtyard to look for J.J. She was pretty sure Skye had been bluffing when she said J.J. was "never gonna be anywhere *but* the bottom. Especially after today." But it wouldn't hurt to warn him. And to stop any CHK who even looked like he was going to give J.J. a hard time —

But she stopped at the top of the steps that led down into the courtyard. J.J. wasn't sitting on the wall waiting for her. In fact, nobody was on the walls. It looked like everyone in the entire school was part of a three-people-deep circle around what appeared to be a performance in progress.

Some kind of school assembly?

No—there was way too much laughing for that. That edgy, rude kind of laughter that meant somebody was at its feet, being kicked around by it.

A chill went through Lucy.

She stood on tiptoes, but even though she was at the top of the steps looking down, she couldn't see exactly what was happening in the center of the circle. At first the noise was confused and muddy, too—until she began to make out some words.

"Cluck, cluck, cluck," male voices were shouting. "Chicken, chicken, chicken."

They weren't just saying them—they were chanting them. Hands were beating on notebooks and backpacks and the empty concrete planters that were supposed to hold shrubs and didn't. Beating on them like drums to the rhythm of "Cluck, cluck, cluck. Chicken, chicken, chicken."

Cluck, Cluck, Cluck ... Lucy gasped and let her soggy sandwich bag drop. Cluck? J.J. Cluck?

"Hey, Cluck Boy!" a deep voice shouted. "Why don't you dance?"

"Yeah," someone else yelled. "You know. Woo-woo-woo or somethin'."

Lucy tore down the steps and shoved her way through the side of the circle. A couple of kids shoved back but she didn't care—not when she elbowed her way to the front and saw J.J., her J.J., being pushed from one big eighth-grade boy to another and back again like a soccer ball. The chant was deafening as the crowd joined in. Lucy could feel it in her chest, though she was sure J.J. wasn't feeling it in his. There was no expression on his face, as if his spirit had left his body to take the abuse. It was the most frightening thing she had ever seen.

"Stop it!" she screamed. "Stop it!"

She tried to hurl herself into the circle, but someone caught her arm and pulled her back. Lucy turned to slap at it and found herself looking into an adult face she didn't recognize at first.

"Slow down," Mr. Lopez said, as calmly as if he were passing out hand-outs in social studies class.

Lucy tried to wrench herself away, but he held on firmly until he could step around her. With his hands over his head he clapped until somebody yelled, "Busted!" and the crowd scattered, their drum beats fading in the air. Both eighth grade boys stepped away from J.J. with the grins still on their faces, and one of them made some kind of signal with his hand behind his back. Lucy watched Ricky and Wolf-Man disappear with the rest of the pack. When she turned her eyes back to what had once been the center of middle school attention, J.J. was gone.

"All right, what's going on?" Mr. Lopez said in his bored voice.

"Nothin,'" one of the boys said.

"Nothing?" Lucy cried. "They were hurting J.J.!"

"Which one's J.J.?" Mr. Lopez said.

"J.J. Cluck," said one of the boys—the one with a moustache starting to grow like flecks of pepper on his upper lip. He made a chicken-clucking sound at the other boy and they both laughed.

"Was anybody hurt?" Mr. Lopez said.

"Nah," was the answer. "We were just messin' with him."

Mr. Lopez sighed. "Well, mess with him someplace else, will you? I don't want any trouble on my watch."

"That's it?" Lucy said as the two boys wandered off, still clucking under their breaths. "That's all you're going to do?"

Mr. Lopez turned and looked at her as if he'd forgotten she was there. "That's all that needs to be done," he said. "You need to choose your battles."

He seemed to want to say her name, but he seemed to have forgotten that, too.

"Don't make something out of nothing," he said. "Kids are going to do that stuff. They're kids."

Lucy opened her mouth to protest, but once again she felt someone grab her arm. This time it was Gabe.

"Let go of me," she said between her teeth as she watched Mr. Lopez walk across the courtyard, through the scattered pieces of trash the students had left.

"I'm walkin' you to class," Gabe said, maneuvering her toward the hall where the Life Skills room was.

"What? I can walk myself."

She pulled her arm away, but Gabe latched onto the strap of her backpack.

"What are you *doing?*" she said.

"Tryin' to keep you from making things worse for the J-Man," he said.

"I'm not making it worse—how could things get any worse?"

Gabe stopped just on the inside of the door and looked down at her with eyes so serious she wasn't sure they were his.

"Yeah, it could," he said. "It could."

He let go then and slipped into the boys' bathroom. But not before Veronica burst from a knot of people waiting to get into their classroom.

"He walked you to class, didn't he?" she said. Her lip was nearly to her chest.

"Yes," Lucy said, "but not like 'walked me' walked me."

Veronica put up a dramatic hand and closed her eyes. "I was all feeling sorry for you this morning because Ms. Pasqual yelled at you, but I'm not any more. I'm over you, Lucy. Done."

Lucy blinked. "What does that mean?"

Veronica's eyes sprang open. "Du-uh—it means we aren't friends any more. You've done the worst thing one girl can do to her friend, and that makes it over. *So* over."

She tossed the ponytail, smacking herself in the face, and flew into the girls' restroom, where Dusty was making an exit. She made a U-turn and followed her in, to the tune of Veronica's wailing.

Maybe Gabe was right. Maybe things *could* get worse.

In Life Skills, the class was supposed to be filling out a worksheet on communication, but all anybody communicated about as far as Lucy could tell was what happened in the courtyard. Texts, notes, and whispers every time Mr. Torres dozed off at his desk filled the hour, although Lucy's messages all came through the dagger eyes of the CHK girls.

The only person not communicating was J.J. He sat with his head on his desk, just the way he used to do all the time before Mr. Auggy came into their life and showed J.J. he was better than that. Lucy had the slipping-away feeling that even Mr. Auggy couldn't show him out of this one.

J.J. wasn't going to let Lucy show him, either, that was clear. At the end of fifth period he sliced his way out of the room before anybody else and didn't wait for her in the hall. When she caught up to him in the pre-algebra room, he was already burying his face in his arms. Lucy slid into the chair beside him at their table.

"You can't let them get to you," she whispered to him.

"They already did," he said without lifting his head.

"Finish up that nap before the bell rings," the Colonel said. "No sleeping in my class."

Lucy held her breath as J.J. sat up. The twitch in his jaw muscle told her to leave it. For now.

Somehow she got through the armpit-drenching experience of solving an equation at the board that period. She didn't think the day was ever going to end. Only the promise of a meeting with Mr. Auggy kept her from breaking every attitude rule she'd ever heard, or running after J.J. when he escaped from the room before the bell was even finished ringing.

"What are we going to tell Veronica?" Dusty whispered to her as they left together.

"Whatever it is, you're going to have to tell her," Lucy said. "She told me I'm not her friend any more."

Dusty gave a deep sigh. "She says that to me about twice a week, 'lillo."

"Why?"

"She's always thinking I want Gabe."

"Nobody wants Gabe!"

"She does. But what do I say to her about this note from Mr. Auggy that she didn't get?"

Lucy blinked at her. "Just tell her that we have a meeting and we'll meet her later at the soccer field."

"We can't do that! It'll *so* hurt her feelings."

Lucy felt a little guilty. She was pretty new to this girlfriend thing. Sometimes the things that hurt somebody's feelings still surprised her. Like, who cared if somebody didn't think your socks were cute or they didn't call you every night when you'd been together all day at school? Or that the kid you had a crush on said a word to some other girl, who you thought was icky?

She was glad to leave that to Dusty, who was very good at it, and caught up with J.J. He was somebody worth worrying about.

"I have to talk to you," she said, "But right now I have to meet Mr. Auggy, so I'll catch up with you—"

J.J. pulled a folded note halfway out of his t-shirt pocket.

"You didn't tell me," Lucy said.

He just grunted.

By the time they got to the front steps of the school, Dusty managed to lose the rest of the team somehow, and Lucy didn't hear Veronica wailing. Mr. Auggy had one leg propped up on the low wall, and he was talking to Gabe.

"Now I'm really confused," Lucy said.

"I hope we're not in trouble," Dusty said.

Lucy and J.J. both looked at her.

"Give me a break, Dusty," Lucy said. "You never get in trouble."

"Hey, thanks for coming," Mr. Auggy said, with his usual small smile. "I wanted to talk to you guys alone before practice, so they let me out of school early." His eyes twinkled. "It's not half as much fun over there at Elementary without you guys."

"Course not," Gabe said.

"So, look, I have a special favor to ask of you three." He pointed to Gabe and Dusty and J.J. "You know Miss Lucy is trying out for the ODP."

"She's totally gonna make it," Dusty said.

"I heard it's not that easy," Gabe said.

Lucy wrinkled her nose at him.

"It's not," Mr. Auggy said, "and I want her to have the best chance possible. She'll get that if I train her with the best people I have." He stuck his hands in his pockets. "So what do you say?"

"Us?" Dusty said. "I mean, you want *me*?"

"You're our best sweeper," Lucy said.

"Well, I can totally see how you'd want me," Gabe said. "I'd try out myself, but I have a pretty busy social schedule."

J.J. gave another grunt.

"What's that J-Man?" Gabe said.

He got J.J. in a head lock, and Lucy saw J.J. almost smile as he wriggled free. It made her want to cry.

"It's going to mean giving up some of your free time," Mr. Auggy said. He looked at Gabe. "Could cut into your social life."

"What social life?" Dusty said. "'Ronica broke up with him today."

"I got other women." He looked at Lucy—who gave him the biggest are-you-kidding-me glare she could get onto her face.

"I'll do it," J.J. said. "Whenever."

Lucy immediately forgot how gross Gabe was and breathed out relief. Maybe this was just what J.J. needed to show him he was still who they all knew he was. No matter what those evil—

"An hour after regular practice every day, and Saturday afternoons?" Mr. Auggy said. "Even after the whole team works out all morning?"

"Yes!" Dusty said, and poked Gabe, who said, "Okay, yeah. Will there be food?" He formed a square smile at Lucy. "Wholesome snacks?"

"You're dead," Lucy said.

But she smiled back at him, at all three of them, because they were going to help her get to her dream, and maybe get J.J. back to himself.

There might be angels after all.

8

Aunt Karen, however, definitely wasn't one of the angels.

Lucy knew that, of course, but she got a reminder the minute she walked in the back door after practice that afternoon. Aunt Karen put a pink, grainy-looking protein shake in Lucy's hand and pointed to a big piece of paper on the table.

"I want you to see this schedule I put together," she said.

Lucy looked at the rows and columns and numbers and felt her eyes glaze over.

"I was thinking you should get up an hour earlier than usual and we'll go for a mile run—then you can stretch and shower while I cook your breakfast. Now this page—" Aunt Karen slid another sheet out. "—is a nutritional plan I've worked up. Where would we be without the Internet?"

Eating Inez's *sopapillas*—that's where they would be.

"I have you coming straight home from school so you can have something nutritious to eat before I drive you to the soccer field—"

"No," Lucy said.

Aunt Karen closed her eyes. "Don't start with me, Lucy."

Start what? Lucy could never figure out what that was supposed to mean. 'No' just meant 'no'.

"I ride my bike to practice with J.J.," she said.

"J.J. can ride with us. So can Januarie." Aunt Karen gave her lips a particularly juicy lick. "I'd take the whole team if I had room in my car." She paused, shiny fingernail on the schedule. "I could look into renting a van while I'm here."

"I don't want to ride in a van. I want to ride my bike."

"I'm going to the field anyway to take the drinks and snacks and besides, it's quicker for you to go in a car, which means more time here to have your energy beverage, change into practice clothes—"

Her fingernail was tapping its way down the paper. Aunt Karen had actually scheduled in changes of clothes? If Lucy hadn't been working so hard against the urge to slam a door, she would have laughed.

"I can tell you're going to be stubborn about this," Aunt Karen said, squeezing the bridge of her nose with her fingers. "All right—you can ride your bike—just to show you that I'm willing to compromise."

"What's 'compromise' mean?" Lucy said.

"I give up a few things, you give up a few, and we both end up with something we're happy about."

Lucy took a long pull through the straw in the protein shake, just to keep from saying, 'I'm not happy about *any* of this!' She was never going to hear the end of it from Gabe if Aunt Karen kept showing up with her "wholesome" snacks. And that was just for starters—

"Practice is over at four," Aunt Karen went on.

"Five."

"Since when?"

"Since Mr. Auggy set up a special ODP practice after our regular one."

"He didn't tell me about that."

"You said for *him* to take care of the athletic stuff."

Aunt Karen frowned. "I'll call him. We need to coordinate."

"I need to do my homework," Lucy said, and turned to go.

"I have that scheduled for after supper. I think you need some down time, too. You can get your homework done between 7:00 and 8:30 if you're efficient. I can help you with that."

"You know what?" Lucy said. "You're right about down time. I'm going to go take some now."

After an eyebrow lift, Aunt Karen nodded. "I feel good about that," she said. "We'll finish this over dinner."

Lucy didn't smell anything as she grabbed the phone and left the kitchen. Of course, salad didn't really have a smell.

She closed her bedroom door extra quietly and dialed Dad's number.

His voice mail said he wasn't in and invited her to leave a message, but she just hung up. If Dad called back when she and Aunt Karen were 'on schedule', she wouldn't get to talk to him in private and tell him she didn't know how much longer she was going to be able to keep a good attitude with Aunt Karen planning out her entire life—and couldn't he do something?

Lucy rolled over and pulled her Book of Lists out from under the pillow. Lollipop jumped out of the toy chest and onto the bed, where she waited for Lucy to make a lap and scratch behind her ear with her pen. But Lucy didn't open the Book.

"I don't want to write about Aunt Karen in here any more," she told Lolli in a whisper. "I only want to write about happy stuff."

Lucy tucked the Book back under her pillow. Lollipop gave a disappointed meow.

"I know," Lucy said. "But I can't think of anything happy to write about right now."

But that changed the next morning when J.J. and Januarie were waiting for her to go to Saturday practice. It didn't even matter to her that Januarie started right in whining about how hungry she was, even though J.J. grunted that she'd just had two bowls of cereal.

Januarie thrust out her lower lip. "That isn't enough to give me energy for the day. Aunt Karen says so."

"What would give you energy?" Lucy said.

Januarie gave her a sly look. "A breakfast burrito at Pasco's."

"Like you've got money for that, moron," J.J. said.

"My dad still has an account there," Lucy said. She looked at her watch. "And we got time." She popped Januarie lightly on the head. "My treat—but only one burrito. And juice."

Januarie suddenly seemed to have enough energy for her and about three other nine-year-olds. She bounced ahead of them and J.J. groaned. Lucy did, too, but she smiled to herself. This was going to give her a chance to finally talk to J.J. about what was going on with the evil CHKs.

When they got inside the café, Januarie was already standing on tiptoes at the counter trying to get Felix Pasco's attention, but he was at the other end, red-faced and pointing at Mr. Benitez.

"It is not my fault you're losing business, Benitez!" Feliz was saying in a not-very-quiet voice. "You still run your store like it's the 1950s."

"Bah!" Mr. Benitez said, in an even less quiet voice. His made Lucy want to climb into the ice cream case. He was nasty even when he wasn't in a bad mood, and he was definitely in one today. He was snarling worse than Mudge when you stepped on his tail.

"You don't have to sell out to the corporates," Felix went on, even as Januarie waved a chubby arm to get his attention.

"It's the only thing I know to do!"

"I'll tell you what to do—"

"It's because of people like *you!*"

Lucy took a step backward, into J.J., because Mr. Benitez was looking at her, shoving his finger in her direction.

"What are you talking about, Benitez?" Feliz said. "She's *una muchacha.* Leave her alone!"

But Mr. Benitez was charging down the counter right at Lucy, spitting words just the way that Nina girl did. "You came to my store twice a week—Tuesday and Friday—every week for years. Then suddenly—nothing."

Lucy folded her arms. He could yell at her all he wanted—but she wasn't taking the blame for *this.*

"It's my aunt's fault," Lucy said. "She's doing the grocery shopping while my dad's away, and I don't tell her what to do—trust me."

Mr. Benitez evidently didn't. He stopped a foot from her, his moustache working like he was chewing on it from the inside.

"Where does she shop now?"

"Wal-Mart," Lucy said. "In Alamogordo."

He let out a holler as if she'd just shot him in the face.

"Benitez! Calm down!" Felix said.

He hurried down the other side of the counter and reached over to put his hand on Januarie's head. She was by now practically drooling for her burrito.

"Leave my customers alone," he said. "Go whine someplace else."

"I will not be back, Pasco!" Mr. Benitez cried. Januarie drew back, face scrunched in disgust.

"Fine with me!" Felix shouted back.

Mr. Benitez stormed out. Lucy looked from the slammed door to

Felix, and she could feel J.J. doing the same. Felix closed his eyes and drew in a long breath through his nostrils and fixed a smile on his face that didn't fool Lucy for a second. Why did grown-ups smile when it was the last thing they wanted to do?

"All right, then, *mi muchachas*," he said after he'd opened his eyes. "What can I do for you this morning?"

"I want a breakfast burrito," Januarie said.

"Please," Lucy put in.

"Please. And an orange juice. Please."

Some of the smile faded from Felix's lips. "May I speak with you, Lucita?" he said.

Lucy got a queasy feeling in her stomach as she followed Felix to the other end of the counter. When they got there, he leaned his forearms on the top and whispered, "Do you have money with you?"

"Money?" Lucy said. "What about my dad's account?"

"Then you didn't know. I didn't want to embarrass you in front of your friends—"

"Know what?" Lucy said.

"That the account is closed."

Lucy felt her eyes bug out. "My dad didn't tell me he did that!"

"He didn't." Felix looked down at his hands.

"It was my Aunt Karen, wasn't it?" Lucy said.

"I told her that was not what Senor Ted would want, but she insisted."

He didn't have to tell her. Lucy could just hear her aunt now, informing Felix that his food wasn't good enough for her. Just like Mr. Benitez's and Inez's. She wondered if she should call Winnie the State Lady and tell her she was being starved in her own home.

"Ah," Felix said, pulling Lucy back from the edge of smacking somebody. "But there are a few dollars left in the account that *su tia* didn't know about. Just enough for a breakfast burrito and three juices."

Felix winked at her, his eye misty with tears. Felix cried a lot for a man.

"Does *tia* mean Evil One?" Lucy said.

"No. It means 'aunt.'"

"Oh," Lucy said. "Same thing."

There was barely time for Felix to fix a burrito-to-go for Januarie before they had to fly off to the soccer field. She still didn't have a chance to talk to J.J., especially since regular practice led right into ODP practice when the others were gone. But after five minutes, all thoughts of the CHKs melted away and she felt like she had wings.

Even though Mr. Auggy had her use only her weaker foot, the left one, for everything—dribbling, shooting, receiving, juggling. He said it would make her a two-footed player.

And even when he challenged her and J.J. to make six passes in a row without Gabe or Dusty touching the ball. And then changed her partner. And then changed it again. He said that would make her a versatile player.

Even when he made her practice a diving header over and over even though it scared her half to death to throw her arms out in front of her and dive toward a low ball and meet it with her forehead—because he said that would make her a fearless player.

And even when, in one-on-one, he wouldn't let her take a turn at being a goalie and she was panting like a cocker spaniel when he finally blew the whistle—because he said that would make her a tireless player.

By the time practice was over and the clouds were gearing up for a pink and orange sunset, she was a wiped-out player.

"How's everybody holding up?" Mr. Auggy said when they were all chugging the water Aunt Karen had left them after regular practice.

Thank heaven she hadn't stayed after everybody got their granola bars.

"I wish the bleachers weren't all apart so we'd have a place to sit down," Dusty said. "Are they ever gonna get fixed?"

Gabe wiped his drippy mouth with the back of his hand and left a smear of dirt. Ew, Lucy thought—although at least he wasn't all over her today.

"My dad told me it ain't gonna happen," Gabe said. "Not as long as the town's still fighting over whether to sell out to that big corporate thing."

"Those people just need to get along," Dusty said. "Can't you have Lucy talk to them, Mr. Auggy?"

Lucy shook her head. After what she'd seen in the café that morning, she'd have better luck talking to Lollipop and Marmalade.

The corners of Mr. Auggy's mouth twitched. "I have no doubt Miss Lucy could get something going," he said. "But right now let's focus on the tryouts. Everybody doing okay? I didn't work you too hard?"

"Dude, I coulda gone two more hours," Gabe said. "How 'bout you, J-Man?"

"Three," J.J. said. It was almost like he'd forgotten about yesterday.

Dusty slumped her shoulders. "Then I'm a wimp, 'cause I only think I could do one more."

Lucy grinned at all of them.

"Okay, you guys jam," Mr. Auggy said. "I need to talk to Miss Lucy."

"Jam?" Gabe said. "I'd prefer peanut butter."

"You are so not funny," Dusty told him.

As their voices trailed off, Mr. Auggy rested his eyes on Lucy. "How about you?" he said. "Did I work you too hard?"

"No!"

"Then let's do a few more drills."

"Okay."

"Listen, Captain." He parked the soccer ball on his hip. "I don't want to push them too hard because they're doing this for the fun of helping you, and if it gets to be a drag they won't want to do it."

"You're about to say 'but'," Lucy said.

"But I have to push *you*, further than you think you can go, because that's what it's going to take just to show up at the tryouts."

Lucy nodded, but she felt a small knot in her stomach. Mr. Auggy was being way more serious than usual.

"I don't want you to lose the joy of the game," he said.

"Yeah, my dad says if it stops being fun, something's wrong."

"He's right. But we have to find out just how far you can go before that happens, because that's what *they're* going to find out the first day."

"Okay," Lucy said.

"Are you sure?"

"Of course I'm sure. It's all I ever wanted to do!"

"Sure enough to maybe want to pull out my nose hairs with red hot tweezers now and then?"

"I'm not gonna want to do that! Ew!"

Mr. Auggy didn't smile. "If you don't get that urge at least once, I'm not doing my job." He cocked his head. "Are you willing to take a chance?"

She didn't tell him he was nuts if he thought she could ever think that.

"Yeah?" he said.

"No *doubt*," Lucy said.

The small smile reappeared. "You have to promise me one thing, Miss Lucy."

"Anything."

"Hear it first. I want you to promise that if at any time you decide this is not what you really want to do, you'll say so. You won't think you have to go ahead with it just so that somebody else won't be disappointed."

Lucy put her hand up and said, "I promise," and then shook her head.

"What?" Mr. Auggy said.

"I thought you were going to make me promise something hard," she said.

Mr. Auggy nodded toward the field. "Then let's get in another half hour."

Lucy grabbed the ball and took off running, and once again she had wings. Because this was one thing she was always, always going to want — more than anything.

9

It was easier not to miss Dad as long as Lucy was concentrating on soccer, but on Sunday, all the homesickness for him rose up like the stomach flu. Sunday was always their day together. *This* Sunday, it was all Aunt Karen, all the time.

In the first place, she made Lucy wear "one of those cute little outfits I bought you," when they went to church. It was green and had puffed sleeves and it itched under the arms and even Dusty whispered to her, "It's not you, is it?" Veronica still wasn't talking to her at all.

Then during the service, as Lucy's mind was wandering through the sermon about seeds and weeds and other stuff that Inez could have explained to her but Reverend Servidio couldn't, she noticed that Felix Pasco and Gloria, who owned Casa Bonita Hair Salon, and Mayor Rosa were sitting on one side of the church, and Mr. Benitez and Claudia, of Claudia's House of Flowers 'n' Candy, and Sheriff Navarra were sitting on the other side. They were all stiff and kept giving each other dark looks across the aisle like the CHKs in the cafeteria. Lucy wasn't surprised.

"People weren't very friendly today," Aunt Karen said when they were walking home, she in teetery heels that tapped importantly on the brick sidewalk.

"They're mad at each other because of the soccer field," Lucy said. "Pasco's side won't sell their businesses to the Mini-Mart people and Mr. Benitez's side wants to."

"What is the big deal?" Aunt Karen said.

Lucy bit her lip for a second so she wouldn't say, *You're* part of the big deal. Instead she said, "If they sell, that means they promise to vote for the town to sell the soccer field, too, and then they'll build a stupid gas station there."

"This town needs a total face lift anyway. Not that it's going to matter to you once you go to ODP." Aunt Karen put her arm around Lucy's shoulder. "I don't think you have any idea how much that's going to change your life."

Lucy pretended to re-puff her sleeve so Aunt Karen would move her hand. As usual, her aunt did *not* get it. At all.

Not only that, but she decided they should go to Cloudcroft for lunch instead of to Pasco's café like Lucy and Dad always did. And they couldn't eat at the diner where Lucy and Dad loved to go on the rare occasions when they got up to the mountain town. It had peanut shells all over the floor and stuff written on the walls by cool poets who lived up there. Aunt Karen was having none of it.

They ate at a "cute little place" that offered a menu only rabbits would order from, where Aunt Karen talked the whole time about Lucy staying hydrated and getting enough sleep and maybe getting her hair cut so it would be easier to take care of. Not that Lucy was taking care of it at all right now, Aunt Karen was careful to add.

By the time they got back to Los Suenos, missing Dad was eating a hole inside Lucy. They always went to the radio station after Sunday lunch and Lucy helped him get ready for his Monday show and they talked about things like bobcats and old movies and Mom.

Lucy never liked to talk to Aunt Karen about Mom. She was her sister, but she hadn't known her like Dad did. Even Lucy, who only had her for seven years, knew Mom better than Aunt Karen did. Obviously.

Before Aunt Karen could suggest that they round out their Sunday by painting each other's toenails or something, Lucy looked out the window to send J.J. a signal, and saw him in his front yard. She blinked to make sure she wasn't having some kind of weird vision.

The yard, always piled with old tires and car parts and household appliances, now housed only a bathtub and a large metal drum with smoke coming out of it. Mr. Auggy was dumping an armload of trash into it and smiling his biggest small-smile ever.

Lucy slipped out the front door and crossed the street. J.J. came out from behind the house with an arm full of trash of his own, which he dropped into the fire.

"Wow," Lucy said.

"It's looking good, isn't it?" Mr. Auggy said. "The J-Man is doing a great job."

J.J. kind of shrugged his bony shoulders and said yeah and then turned red because the 'yeah' shot way up into the stratosphere.

"I bet you're looking for somebody to kick a ball around with, aren't you?" Mr. Auggy said to Lucy.

She nodded, because she was still too shocked to even speak. She had never actually seen the ground in front of J.J.'s house before.

"Go ahead if you want, J.J.," Mr. Auggy said. "We're about done here. I have to figure out what to do with this bathtub."

Lucy didn't ask why anybody had a bathtub in their front yard in the first place. "Meet me in ten," Lucy said to J.J., and dashed back to her yard.

J.J. arrived in five, and he was glowering—because Januarie followed him in through the gate. Then Lucy glowered, because Aunt Karen came out the back door and sat on the top step and patted it for Januarie to join her. Januarie scurried to her, face lit up like the top of a birthday cake.

"How cozy," Lucy muttered to J.J.

He just grunted.

They started a game of one-on-one, and Aunt Karen started a conversation. Didn't she know there was no talking in soccer, besides "To me!" and "Wall!" and "Man on!"

"Aunt off!" was more like it.

"So what is your mom doing today?" Aunt Karen said.

"*My* mom?" Januarie said.

J.J. maneuvered the ball farther from the porch with Lucy on him.

"Yeah. I never see her, and I just wondered what she does inside all day."

"She doesn't do anything," Januarie said.

Lucy snagged the ball from J.J. and made a push pass that landed under the patio table. Maybe if she could get close enough she could whisper to Aunt Karen that this was not a good subject to bring up.

But as Lucy bent over to retrieve the ball, Aunt Karen babbled on.

"She must do something. Does she talk on the phone to friends?"

"She doesn't have any friends," Januarie said.

"No! Really? I'm sure she's a nice person—after all, she's *your* mom."

"She makes cookies sometimes."

"See, there you go. Do you think she'd like to come over and have coffee?"

J.J. let the ball roll into a yellowed pile of cottonwood leaves. Lucy turned to see Januarie staring hard at her chubby hands. It took a lot to hush her up, especially around Aunt Karen.

"I like to take a break mid-morning and have a latte," Aunt Karen said. "I think I'll invite her over tomorrow."

Januarie's face came up, and she looked at Lucy as if she were falling down a hole. She could almost hear J.J. gritting his teeth.

"Mrs. Cluck hardly ever comes out of her house," Lucy said for them.

Aunt Karen folded her hands around her knees and rocked back. "And why is that?"

"Because—it's just hard for her right now." At least, that was what Dad told Lucy. Mr. Cluck was mean to J.J.'s mom, too, when he was living there. Dad said she needed time to get over it. Lucy was pretty sure she didn't need Aunt Karen.

"I'm sorry to hear that." Aunt Karen stood up. "Come on, Jan-Jan. Let's go inside and do something with those fingernails. Girl, when was the last time you had a decent manicure?"

"She's nine," Lucy said to J.J. when they'd gone inside the house. "Why would she *ever* have had a manicure?"

"She has to leave my mom alone."

J.J.'s jaw muscles were like a rubber band, poised to be shot across a room.

"Januarie?" Lucy said.

"No."

"Aunt Karen."

"Yeah."

Lucy pretended to practice trapping the ball. "What'll happen if she asks her over?"

J.J. didn't answer for a minute. He snatched up the ball from between her feet and juggled it several times with his calves. Finally he said, "She'll lock herself in her room and Januarie'll get all—"

"Emo," Lucy said.

"Yeah, and then that state lady—"

"Winnie."

"Yeah, she'll come and tell my mom she has to come out so we can be a family."

The jaws clamped down. End of conversation. Lucy was surprised he'd said that much. It was the most he'd ever told her about his mysterious mother. Come to think of it, Lucy hadn't seen her for almost a year.

"So, it's almost like *you* don't have a mother either," Lucy said.

J.J. didn't answer. She didn't expect him to. And she also didn't expect him to talk now about what had happened Friday at school either. They started a game of Knockout and didn't talk at all. Maybe soccer healed things words couldn't.

But she did want to talk to Aunt Karen that night and tell her she should leave Mrs. Cluck alone. Dad called, though—and Lucy still didn't have enough privacy to tell him about Aunt Karen's new schedule for her life. And then Aunt Karen accused Lollipop of running off with her wrist watch—which did not turn out to be true. But by the time all that was over, Lucy decided the J.J.'s mom talk could wait until morning.

Except that at 6:30 a.m., Aunt Karen said Lucy shouldn't waste her breath and energy talking while she was running, which they did before the Sacramento Mountains were even awake. Lucy vowed she'd do it while she was having her cereal—because she'd already told Aunt Karen she wasn't eating scrambled eggs.

But when Lucy opened the pantry, she found a box of Kashi Something or Other where the Captain Crunch should have been.

She turned to Aunt Karen, who was at the table with her coffee and her laptop. Her nails were clicking fast on the keys.

"Where's my cereal?" Lucy said.

"You're holding it."

Lucy stared at the front of the box. Whole grain. Fiber. 18 essential vitamins and minerals. It was sure to taste exactly like Marmalade's cat litter.

"All the sugar in that other junk isn't good for your body," Aunt Karen said. "Now before you start going ballistic on me, look at this." She pointed at her laptop screen.

Making a silent vow to toss the Kashi into the cat box the first chance she got, Lucy looked reluctantly over Aunt Karen's shoulder. OLYMPIC DEVELOPMENT PROGRAM filled the screen in bright blue and orange letters.

"This is the ODP website," Aunt Karen said. "And I am just about to find—" She clicked the mouse and things changed and before Lucy could even get focused on it, she clicked again and said, "Yes! Fred Yancey."

"Who's that?"

"That is our New Mexico ODP coordinator. And *that*—" She clicked again. "—is his contact information."

"I bet Mr. Auggy already has it," Lucy said. "He's doing all that stuff for me." She didn't add that the last time Aunt Karen had anything to do with ODP people, she messed it all up.

"Mr. Auggy's doing a fabulous job," Aunt Karen said to the screen.

Then why do you keep clicking things? Lucy wanted to ask her. But since she couldn't imagine saying it without attitude, she grabbed a banana for breakfast and went down the hall.

"Shower," Aunt Karen said without looking up. "And you will eat more than that before you leave this house."

It wasn't until Lucy saw J.J. at the gate that she remembered about his mother, and she swallowed a big lump of guilt, along with the Kashi that was still hanging out in her esophagus. It was hard to digest food when you were snarling to yourself. But J.J. wasn't clamping his jaw, so Lucy decided to leave it alone for now.

Nobody else was leaving anything alone, however.

"Guess what?" Carla Rosa said as they were all crossing the street toward the school. There was the slightest hint of a nip in the air, so Carla was wearing the white knit cap with the big sequins on it which she probably wouldn't take off until the temperature hit 90 degrees again.

"I don't know, C.R., what?" Gabe said.

Oscar poked Emanuel. "Who's C.R.?"

"Carla Rosa, moron," Emanuel said.

"What, Carla Rosa?" Lucy said, before that started a smack-down in the middle of First Street.

"You already know. I'm talking to Veronica and Oscar and Emanuel."

"Okay, *what?*" Veronica said. Judging from the way she was swinging that ponytail as she walked, she was obviously in a worse mood than usual even for a Monday morning.

"Mr. Auggy's making a special team," Carla Rosa said, "and we're not on it."

"That ain't true," Oscar said. He looked at Emanuel. "Is it?"

Emanuel shrugged. He'd already used up all his words for the day.

Veronica's lower lip drooped. "So—who *is* on it?"

"It's not a special team," Dusty said.

"You're on it? And you didn't tell me?"

"Here comes the emo," Gabe said.

"And you?"

Gabe gave his eyebrows a wicked wiggle. "If there's a special team, you better believe I'm gonna be on it."

"They're just helping me get ready for the ODP tryouts," Lucy said as Veronica's lip sank toward her belly button.

"Why can't we help?" Oscar said.

"Because guess what—we're not good enough."

Oscar glared at Carla Rosa. "Speak for yourself."

"Now I feel like even more of a loser than I did already," Veronica wailed, looking straight at Lucy.

Gabe grinned. "Maybe you are a—"

"Okay, look," Lucy said. "Nobody's a loser. Mr. Auggy just asked J.J. and Dusty and Gabe to help me get ready for the tryouts, but that doesn't mean we aren't all still a team. Hello—we have a game this Saturday!"

"With the meanest team in life," Dusty said. "So we have to stick together and get ready."

They stopped at the bottom of the school's front steps. Veronica twisted her arms in front of her like two strands of cooked pasta.

"I don't think I want to play," she said.

"Don't bother."

Lucy groaned inside. That voice was becoming way too familiar. Nina. Which meant Skye couldn't be too far away.

Lucy turned to face them, and saw Ricky and Wolf-Man, too. Together they all looked like the cover of some CD she wouldn't want to listen to. The vision of J.J. being clucked at flashed through her mind. Nuh-uh—that wasn't happening again.

"Could you excuse us?" she said. "We're having a team meeting."

Skye opened her mouth, but Wolf-Man cut in front of her. His eyes were slits like paper cuts, and Lucy was sure his tongue was going to flick out, lizard-like, any second.

"It's not gonna do you any good," he said. "You might as well forfeit now because we are gonna take you down."

Lucy followed his reptile eyes. He was looking straight at J.J.

Gabe huffed. "You four?"

"You haven't seen the rest of the team," Skye said.

"Are you talking about those imbeciles who were doing the chicken dance in the courtyard Friday?" Lucy said.

"Yeah," Ricky said—and then looked as if he weren't sure that was the right answer.

Lucy sniffed. "If that's your team, I don't think we have anything to worry about."

Ricky jerked a look at Wolf-Man, but he was zeroed in on J.J. as if the rest of them weren't even there.

"So," Lucy said, "we're done. We'll see you Saturday."

"Oh, you'll see us before then."

Wolf-Man took a step toward J.J., who didn't back up, though Lucy saw his jaw clamp down. At his sides, his fists were clenching and unclenching. Lucy's stomach went into a double knot.

"What does that mean?" Gabe said. "You throwin' a pre-game party or somethin'?"

"That sounds cool," Veronica said.

She gave a weak giggle no one paid any attention to. Ricky was still staring J.J. down, with Wolf-Man edging up behind him. J.J.'s fists stayed clenched this time.

"If I were givin' a party," Wolf-Man said, "I wouldn't be invitin' any half-breeds. I don't serve their kind."

Lucy hauled in a breath and let it out with a loud *BUZZZZZ* as she sliced between Wolf-Man and J.J. They both had to step back or smash her.

"What's with the buzzing?" Ricky asked.

"That's what we do on our team when somebody gets all up in someone else's face," Lucy said. "It reminds them to stop acting like a moron."

Someone growled, and since Lucy wasn't sure whether it was Wolf-Man or J.J., she put out her palms to give them both a push. Before she even touched either one of them, a voice said, "Don't go there."

Heads snapped around and bodies froze. The Colonel was at the top of the steps, hands parked on his hips, eyes riveted. Surrounding kids scattered, leaving only the sound of Carla Rosa whispering, "Guess what? We're in trouble."

The Colonel took the steps down one by one and swung his arms stiffly at his sides, chopping the air.

"You have a bone to pick with these people, Wolfgang?" he said.

Who was he talking to?

Wolf-Man shook his head.

"I don't believe I heard you."

"No, sir," Wolf-Man said.

The Colonel bulleted his eyes at J.J. "How about you? Do you have a problem with Wolfgang?"

"Who's Wolfgang?" Oscar mumbled.

Gabe put his hand over Oscar's mouth. This would definitely not be the time to laugh.

"You don't even know who you're picking a fight with?" the Colonel said. "Jedediah, meet Wolfgang. Wolfgang, Jedediah."

They both nodded like they would rather have been eating broccoli.

"Shake hands like men."

"Dude—" Wolf-Man said.

"I said shake hands!"

Lucy would have jumped over the railing if he'd told her to in that tone. As it was, she slid out from between them. J.J. stuck out his hand and Wolf-Man touched it like it was a hot poker and jerked away.

"Now that you two know each other," the Colonel said, "you can discuss your differences like gentlemen instead of a couple of gang-bangers—which we don't tolerate around here. Is that understood?"

Wolf-Man mumbled something.

"Do I need to get you to the speech therapist, Wolfgang?" the Colonel said. "Speak up. Do you understand what I just said to you?"

Wolf-Man shoved his hands into his pockets and twisted his mouth all sideways and looked everywhere but at the Colonel. His dad obviously hadn't given him any attitude rules. The rest of them stood there looking like they'd rather be anywhere else until Wolf-Man finally gave a tight-sounding "Yes."

The 's' hissed out but the Colonel let it go and turned toward J.J. Before he could speak, Lucy said, "Our team understands, too. Right, Dreams?"

There was a unanimous nod. J.J.'s was barely visible.

The Colonel gave Lucy a very long look. She stopped breathing. *Please, please, please—don't make J.J. talk right now.*

"All right," the Colonel said finally. "Let's muster." When no one moved, he said, "That means get to class."

The CHKs were the first to split, even before the Colonel marched back up the steps. The Dreams waited until the door closed behind him before they melted into a puddle.

"Okay, first of all," Veronica said, "*Wolfgang?*"

"I wouldn't be callin' him that," Gabe said. He puffed up his chest. "I mean, I would, but I don't want to have to deck him."

Cara Rosa shook her head. "Guess what? If you fight him you'll get in trouble with that teacher."

"The good thing is, the Coyote Kids are scared of the Colonel, too," Dusty said. "I don't think they're going to hassle us any more after that."

"Nah," Gabe said, grinning, "It's me they're scared of."

Lucy looked up at the doors. Four faces looked back through the glass. Skye and Nina had their upper lips curled into their nostrils, and Ricky was snapping his chin up and down in a taunt. Wolf-Man's eyes had disappeared into their snake-slits.

The Coyote Kids weren't scared of anybody, and Lucy was pretty sure this was just the beginning of the hassles. For the time being, though, she'd steered trouble away from J.J.

She looked for him now as the rest of the team hurried up the steps to "muster." He was standing at the steel railing, bouncing his fist off of it. When she got to him, he didn't look at her.

"You okay?" she said.

"No."

"Maybe they know they can't just walk on us now," Lucy said, though she sounded more sure than she was.

"Not us. You."

"Huh?"

J.J. pulled away from the railing. "Nothin'," he said.

With jaw clenched, he made his lanky way up the steps. Conversation over before it started. Lucy followed him, but inside herself, she wasn't quite sure where they were going.

10

Lucy was right about one thing. The hassles had only just begun.

From the way the teachers clamped down that day, she was pretty sure the Colonel had gone straight to the faculty lounge before the bell rang and ordered them all to cut no one any slack. Even Mr. Torres barked at the class third period, and Ms. Pasqual all but pulled out a bull whip and snapped it over their heads during study hall.

That didn't stop the CHKs—including the Queen B's—from shooting looks sharp as arrows at the Dreams and bumping into them in the halls between classes and saying "buzzzz" under their breaths.

"I wish you hadn't told them about our buzz thing, Lucy," Dusty said at the lunch table. "They've ruined it for us."

"Would you rather I'd just let Wolfgang push J.J. down the steps?" Lucy said.

J.J. shoved himself up from the table and snatched up his backpack. He cut three people off as he knifed his way from the cafeteria.

"Guess what?" Carla Rosa said. "He's mad."

"Ya think?" Oscar said, punching Emanuel.

Gabe looked at Lucy. "I told you, Lucy Goosey."

Veronica was immediately at attention. "Told her what?" Veronica said.

Gabe went back to his pizza

"What did you tell her that you didn't tell me?"

Lucy abandoned her lunch and grabbed her stuff and left them to sort that out. Her heart was pounding by the time she found J.J. in the still-empty courtyard.

"They're already dead, J.J." Lucy said, pointing to the fallen cottonwood leaves he was tearing up.

He grunted.

"Why are you mad?" Lucy said.

"Leave it," he said. "Just—just leave it."

Lucy shook her head. "You'll let it all build up and then you'll explode at the wrong time and get in trouble."

"Then let me," he said, and hurried out of the courtyard.

He didn't talk to Lucy for the rest of the school day and she didn't push him. That was one thing she knew about J.J. That made her feel lonely and less like herself, and by the time sixth period was over, she was ready to get away from there and play soccer and be real.

"I'll see you guys at the field," Lucy told Dusty and Veronica at the lockers. "I have to check in with Inez first."

"Okay," Dusty said.

Veronica kept her head buried in her locker, between the mirror and the hoodie on a hook.

"You're coming, right, 'Ronica?" Dusty said.

"Maybe."

Lucy closed the door on her own undecorated locker. "You're not still mad about the ODP thing, are you?"

"It's not just that," Veronica said.

Or at least, that's what Lucy thought she said. It was hard to understand somebody who was talking into a stack of colored binders. Dusty pulled her out by the strap of her girly–dress.

"I'm sort of over that." Veronica gave Lucy a withering look. "And I'm almost over the you and Gabe thing."

"There is no 'me and Gabe' thing!"

"As long as you tell him to back off when he flirts with you."

"He doesn't flirt with me—ick!"

"Then you promise?"

Lucy rolled her eyes. "Yes—whatever."

Veronica nodded, but she still had her shoulders up to her ears.

"Then what *else* is the matter?" Dusty said.

"I don't want to play in a game with—" Veronica shifted her

eyes around—"those Coyote Hills kids," she whispered. "You know they're going to try something on the field."

Dusty wrinkled her brow. "Would they do that, *'lillo?*"

Lucy hitched her backpack over her shoulder. "They could try, but they won't get away with it. Remember at camp this summer? The way the rules are, it's, like, almost impossible to cheat. And if you do, refs catch everything. Nobody even plays dirty for more than, like, five seconds."

Dusty nudged Veronica with her message bag. "See?"

"Maybe," Veronica said.

"We'll see you at the field," Dusty said with a smile for Lucy.

But all the way home, Lucy felt like there was a burr under her backpack. Mr. Auggy always said soccer was 'the beautiful game'. Soccer people were good people. Soccer could bring people together, even people who couldn't stand each other, and so it could change the world.

Maybe the CHKs didn't get that memo.

And maybe Lucy needed to deliver it.

She stopped at the top of her back steps. Whoa. Where had *that* come from? Was that like an angel swooping in with a message?

Lucy hoped not. How was she supposed to even talk to the Howl players now? If she said a word to them at school, she'd be in trouble with the Colonel. J.J. would tell her to leave it. Even Gabe was warning her to back off, when he usually didn't care what she did.

Lucy toed at some leaves that had fallen from the elder tree. There was no way to confront them at school—but she couldn't just stand by and let them ruin soccer, either. Could she do anything about it *on* the soccer field?

She would have given that a longer thought, except that through the window in the door she could see Aunt Karen standing at the counter next to Inez, giving new meaning to the term 'getting all up in somebody's dental work.' Lucy charged in.

"You need to go clean that up," Aunt Karen was saying, "and when you're done, see what you can do about this. I've about had it with that animal—"

"What animal?" Lucy said.

Aunt Karen didn't look up from the white sweater she was waving around. "That cat."

"The black one," Mora said from the table.

"What happened?"

"She left something disgusting on the rug in my room and on my cashmere sweater—"

"Hairball," Mora said. "It was nasty."

"If he—"

"She," Mora said.

"—puts a paw in my room again, so help me—"

"Where is she?" Lucy said.

"Locked in the bathroom, where she can stay as long as I'm here."

Lucy started in that direction.

"So—what are you going to use to clean that rug, Inez?" Aunt Karen said. "If it sits there like that it's going to stain."

Her voice was so pointy it went through Lucy. It must feel like a red hot skewer going into Inez. Lucy turned around, mouth open to protest, but Inez caught her eye and ever so slightly shook her head.

"What does that mean?" Aunt Karen said to Inez. "Are you or are you not the maid?"

"She's the nanny," Lucy said, and she didn't care about her tone.

"Senorita Lucy." Inez's voice was so low, Lucy could hardly hear it. "See to Senorita Kitty."

Lucy made it into the bathroom this time and rescued Lollipop from behind the toilet. Her paws went around Lucy's neck as she carried her to the bedroom, where Mora was already waiting.

"Okay," she said the second Lucy had the door closed. "I used to really think your Aunt Karen was cool—"

"I didn't," Lucy said. She deposited the kitty into the toy chest and watched her curl into an angry ball in the corner. Lucy wished she could do the same thing.

"But ever since she came here to live—"

"She doesn't live here."

100

"—I don't like her that much any more." Mora sat up, cross-legged, on the bed, and made some punctuation mark in the air Lucy was sure even Mrs. Huntington had never seen. "I can totally understand her being all mad about her sweater. I mean, it *is* cashmere. But she didn't have to be mean to Abuela."

"I know."

"Abuela doesn't like it either, I can tell."

Lucy sank onto the giant stuffed soccer ball beside her bed, and her stomach knotted. "She isn't going to quit, is she?"

"Are you kidding? Abuela totally loves you." Mora rolled her huge eyes. "She treats you way better than she does me."

"That's because I'm nicer than you," Lucy said.

"Hello!"

"And smarter."

"You *so* are not!"

"And—"

"Shut *up!*"

Mora reached behind her and grabbed Lucy's pillow and threw it at her. The Book of Lists tumbled to the floor.

"I swear I didn't do that on purpose," Mora said, eyes bugging. "Honest. Is it okay?"

Lucy picked it up and brushed it off tenderly before she tucked it back under her pillow. "It's fine," she said.

"I know that's like my phone is to me." Mora nodded solemnly. "And don't worry about Abuela. She would never leave you, trust me."

Lucy nodded and looked carefully at Mora. There were actually a few things she *could* trust Mora on.

"Okay," she said, "I have a question."

"*You* have a question for *me?*" Mora said. "What do I know more about than you do? Boys?"

"Yes," Lucy said.

She thought Mora's eyes were going to burst out of their sockets.

"Are you *serious?* Oh, my gosh! You like somebody? Is it J.J.? No—you wouldn't be asking me about him—you know everything about him—"

"Mora—hush up or I'm not even going to ask you."

Mora clapped her hand over her mouth, eyes still popping, and motioned with her hand for Lucy to go on.

"All I want to know," Lucy said, "is how to get a boy to leave you alone when he's all flirting with you—or somebody else thinks he's flirting with you and you don't want her mad at you—"

"Because she likes him," Mora said, nodding as if she already knew the whole story.

"Right. And she can have him, as far as I'm concerned."

"So you don't like him as a boyfriend?"

"No! He's icky!"

Mora leaned in and whispered, "Is it that Oscar kid?"

"No! It's Gabe."

"Gabe?" Mora said, blinking like she had something in her eyes. "Lucy, he's hot."

"Mora—you're not helping me."

"Okay, okay—just because I can't relate doesn't mean I don't know what to do." She held up her hand and began counting off on her fingers. "You have three options. One, you act as hateful as you can to him."

"I can't. I'd get buzzed by Mr. Auggy, and it's not good attitude for ODP."

"Good, because knowing Gabe he'd just try harder. He's that type."

"What's number two?" Lucy said.

"Two—act like you like somebody else."

Lucy just looked at her.

"Never mind. That would be a challenge for Gabe, too. Besides, he'd never believe it, on a number of levels."

Mora seemed about to go into the levels, so Lucy held up three fingers.

"Oh, number three." Mora frowned. "I've never actually tried this, but I've heard it sometimes works, although it isn't as much fun—"

"What is it?"

"You tell him to his face that you don't want to be his girlfriend. Only don't do it mean or he'll turn on you. Boys' egos are very fragile."

Lucy wasn't sure what an ego was, but she didn't think there was anything fragile about Gabe.

"So, how do I do that?" Lucy said.

Mora's eyes took on a sheen. "You make him think it's his idea. You always have to do that with boys, whether you're their girlfriend or not. They don't like it when we're stronger and smarter than they are, even though we usually are."

Lucy was more confused than ever. Coming to Mora was a mistake.

"Okay, thanks," she said, and headed for the door.

"Where are you going?"

"I'm gonna go clean the rug," Lucy said.

Lucy's hope that soccer practice would make her feel better dwindled about five minutes after they hit the field.

Carla Rosa was back to not being able to dribble the ball more than two inches without losing focus.

Veronica practically burst into tears every time somebody captured the ball from her.

Oscar pretty much gave up defending the goal, and Emanuel didn't even grab Oscar's toothpick and tell him to shape up.

Dusty tried to be all positive with everybody, saying "good try!" when nobody was trying, and "Way to go!" when they hadn't really gone anywhere.

Lucy did her best to direct the team like she was supposed to, as captain and as midfielder. But only Dusty seemed to be listening, and although Gabe paid attention, it was only to tickle her in the ribs every time she got close to him—which only made Veronica shoot bullets with her eyes.

Lucy could have played through all of that if it hadn't been for J.J. He wasn't talking to her, except for the occasional grunt that didn't count as talking even for him. Worse than that, he wouldn't even look at her, no matter how many times she passed him the ball or yelled, "To me, J.J.!" At ODP practice, she even tried deliberately fouling him, just to get him to show that he knew she was on the field. All she got was another grunt. When practice was over, he shot off on his bike alone.

"Boys can just be stupid sometimes, *'lillo,"* Dusty said. "Don't worry."

That was sort of like saying, 'Don't breathe.' Lucy wouldn't have been able to think about anything else, except that the CHKs demanded a lot of attention.

As the week went on, Lucy had to admit they were good at being evil without letting the grown-ups know what was going on.

In Mrs. Huntington's English class, Ricky "accidentally" knocked J.J.'s vocabulary homework off his desk and Wolf-Man stepped on it, leaving a large footprint right in the middle.

In social studies, the Queen B's waited until Mr. Lopez was facing the map on the wall before one of them distracted J.J. while the other one took the orange colored pencil he was using to color in mountain ranges and drew pictures of chickens with it.

In science it was much easier for the CHKs. Nina and Skye could sit right in front of J.J. and text message back and forth in big letters that said HALF-BREED over and over.

There wasn't much they could do in study hall except deliver black looks at him until Lucy herself was ready to explode. Somehow J.J. managed to appear to be ignoring it all, at least to them. But Lucy knew the taut jaw and the balled up fists and the quiet and the stillness were signs of what threatened beneath his skin.

Yet there was nothing she could do at school, and J.J. wouldn't talk about any kind of after-school plan. The only thing that kept her from crumbling was that he was still coming to ODP practice, even though he didn't have to. So she just kept telling herself they could somehow work it out on the soccer field. On Saturday.

But the tension kept melting over into after-school practices. It reminded Lucy of the juice from the broccoli running into the applesauce on your plate and messing up the whole meal.

Finally, at Wednesday's practice, after Aunt Karen left with the cooler and took Januarie with her, Mr. Auggy gathered them next to the used-to-be bleachers. J.J. gave a pile of wood a kick and sent some splinters skittering across the ground.

"What's up, Dreams?" Mr. Auggy said, without his small smile, without any smile at all. "You're looking a little more like a nightmare out there."

"I'm sick of bein' bossed around." Gabe wasn't wiggling his eyebrows or grinning his wicked grin. He wasn't looking at Lucy either, to her surprise.

"Miss Lucy's midfielder," Mr. Auggy said. "She can see the whole field—it's her job to give you a heads up."

"I'm not talkin' about her," Gabe said. He toed one of the shards of wood J.J. had knocked off.

Mr. Auggy scanned the group with his eyes. Veronica started crying.

"Guess what?" Carla Rosa said. "We don't want to play that other team because they do mean stuff."

"How do you know that if we've never played them?" Mr. Auggy said.

Everybody looked at Lucy, who looked at J.J. His eyes met hers for the first time in days. They clearly said, "Leave it."

"They talk trash about how they're going to take us down," Lucy said carefully.

"Teams do that sometimes—just messing with your heads." Mr. Auggy swept his eyes over them. "Is that all?"

"Guess what?" Carla Rosa said.

"Okay, so they talk tough," Gabe said. "Big deal."

"Do we have to play them, though, Mr. Auggy?" Veronica said. Her voice was clogged with tears.

"It's bad form to break a commitment to a game. Especially right now." He picked up a chunk of the bleacher. "You know the town is split in half over your field. If you back out of a game, guess which side wins?"

Lucy could almost see Mr. Benitez scowling his eyebrows down to his nose and refusing to buy them any more uniforms. And Claudia no longer ordering chocolate soccer balls for Game Day. At the thought of never even *having* another Game Day, her stomach tied into a knot again.

"Guess what?" Carla Rosa said. "I don't want to get hurt."

"And you think that's going to happen?" Mr. Auggy said.

Dusty put one arm around Veronica and one around Carla Rosa. "We're scared, Mr. Auggy," she said.

J.J. grew still. Oscar and Emanuel had stopped chewing their toothpicks.

"Then there is only one thing to do," Mr. Auggy said. "Send them a message."

Gabe nudged J.J. and shoved his sleeves up. "Now that's what I'm talkin' about."

"Not that kind of message."

"A text message?" Dusty said.

"I don't got a phone," Oscar said.

Mr. Auggy put a hand up. "We send a message that we won't play dirty. And we do it in our own language."

"Spanish?" Veronica said. "Lucy doesn't speak Spanish. Neither does J.J."

A light came on in Lucy's head. A light that had started to flicker days ago, and had been snuffed out by Aunt Karen bossing Inez around and exiling Lollipop to the bathroom and J.J. and Veronica not speaking to her. "Are you talking about soccer language?" she said.

Mr. Auggy's small smile returned. "Absolutely. Circle up."

Faces looked befuddled, but the team got into a ring. Mr. Auggy juggled the ball while he explained: "As I pass you the ball, I'm going to give you a rule. You have to repeat the rule as you pass it, and the person you pass it to does the same until everybody has said it. Then you give the ball back to me and I give you a new rule. Got it?"

"Got it," Lucy said, before Carla Rosa could say that, guess what, she didn't get it.

"Don't play dirty just because they are," he said with a soft pass to Veronica.

Then it was: "The harder they play dirty, the harder you play clean."

Next: "No arguing with officials. Only the captain discusses problems with the ref."

And, finally, "After the game is over, let it go."

When they were finished, Gabe juggled the ball and J.J. tried to get it and they both looked tight-faced, the way Lucy had figured out boys did when they actually didn't understand something. Amazingly, it was Oscar who spoke for them.

"So, Mr. A," he said with a clean toothpick in his mouth.

"Yeah, Mr. Oscar."

"How's that gonna keep them Howls from playin' dirty?"

"It might not," Mr Auggy said, "but it'll keep *you* from playing dirty. And guess what?" He grinned at Carla Rosa. "Right now, that's all I care about."

Of course, he cared about more than that at the ODP practice that took place right after that. It seemed to Lucy that what he cared about was making scoring a goal as hard as it could possibly be.

He put two cones about three feet in from each of the goalposts, and with Gabe as goalie — which made him practically lick his chops at the chance to thwart all of Lucy's shots — and J.J. and Dusty taking turns guarding her, Lucy had to try to score. But the only goals that counted were the ones that went between the cones.

In fifteen minutes she only got one ball in, and that was by faking Gabe out and catching him at the wrong side of the box.

The diving header she attempted was the worst disaster. When she threw her arms out in front of her and dove toward the ball like Mr. Auggy said, it banged into the top of her head. She lay there, stunned, and Gabe almost stepped on her as his momentum carried him forward.

"Meet the ball with your forehead," Mr. Auggy said as he reached a hand down to her. "Oh, and get up immediately so you don't get kicked."

"Uh, hello!" she said.

He grinned. "How about a break?"

"I'm glad I wasn't the one trying to score," Dusty said. "That was way hard."

"I'm teaching Miss Lucy how to aim for the edges," Mr. Auggy said.

As the other three went for the water bottles Aunt Karen had left for them, he cocked his head at Lucy. "I was also teaching you to deal with the limitations of a dynamite goalie who won't let you shoot down the middle, which can be frustrating. How's that workin' for you?"

Lucy grinned. "I don't want to pull out your nose hairs with red hot tweezers yet."

He grinned back. "Then I guess I'm not working you hard enough yet. And Miss Lucy?"

"Uh-huh." Lucy shook back the wisps of hair that had snuck out of her ponytail and were now plastered to her face.

"Everybody has to play by those rules. Not just you."

"Okay."

He tossed her the ball. "Okay—let's work on those diving headers."

J.J. left his water bottle and jogged back out onto the field. Lucy wished it were that simple everywhere else.

11

Okay, So God: Why Doesn't It Seem Like Game Week — and What Am I Supposed To Do About It?

That was the longest title in the short history of the Book of Lists. But as Lucy scratched the top of Lollipop's head with her pen, she figured a bummer this big deserved a huge headline.

1. Mayor Rosa didn't declare this Pride in Los Suenos Week like he always does when we have a game on Saturday. I asked Carla Rosa why and she said, guess what, he gets mad every time she talks about it. How come grown-ups can get mad when they don't want to talk about something, but kids have to talk about it anyway? Everybody except J.J.

2. Nobody's announced our game on the radio because Dad isn't here.

Which was the hardest reason why it didn't seem like Game Week. Dad always got so proud and called her Champ and had Felix Pasco sit next to him at the game so he could tell him what was going on. She went back to the List before the knot in her stomach could tighten any more.

3. Veronica and Dusty's moms haven't made any banners to hang up on Granada Street and over Highway 54 so everybody knows we're playing in Coyote Hills. Maybe Mayor Rosa and the Town Council won't let them.

Maybe Mr. Benitez won't sell them any groceries if they do. They could all learn a thing or two from Mr. Auggy's rules. Like don't play dirty because somebody else is.

Lollipop jumped from the bed before Lucy could write the next thing and went to the closed bedroom door and meowed.

"You can't go out, Lolli," Lucy said. "Aunt Karen'll lock you in the bathroom."

Lollipop had already been sent there once that day for digging Aunt Karen's used floss out of the trash can and chewing on it. Aunt Karen said that was totally gross and she didn't think it was funny when Lucy said Lolli was just working on her dental hygiene.

Though Lolli continued to insist, Lucy went back to the Book of Lists. This was her scheduled "down time" and she only had a few minutes to finish before Bible study. Right now, Inez was busy serving coffee to Aunt Karen and a guest in the living room. Like Aunt Karen couldn't pour coffee for herself and Whoever.

4. The Dreams aren't all, "Hey, we're gonna do our best to play a beautiful game." We're just trying to remember to play cleaner and harder and keep our mouths shut and let it go. I think there's gonna be a lot to let go.

There was a tap on the door, and before Lucy could say, "Don't let the cat out!" Mora opened it and Lollipop dashed from the room.

"Which way did she go?" Lucy said, scrambling from the bed.

"Who?" Mora said. "Abuela says it's time for Bible study." She poked her head in further and lowered her voice so it sounded like she had a sore throat. "She's in a really bad mood, too, so look out."

Inez looked pretty calm to Lucy when they found her at the kitchen table with her hands folded on her open Bible. Of course, she always seemed peaceful when she was about to run her finger down one of its pages and start talking.

But Lucy was still careful to smile at her as she slipped into her chair. She was going to tell her how delicious the *sopapillas* looked, too, but there weren't any. The plate that usually held their warm, sweet puffiness was covered with celery sticks and carrot curls and little bouquets of raw broccoli and cauliflower. Lucy didn't even see any ranch dressing to dip them in. She decided to forget about having a snack.

"We will see about Senorita Mary," Inez said.

Lucy scooted in on her chair so she could hear over Aunt Karen's voice going on and on in the living room. Whoever she was talking to didn't have much to say. Lucy wondered if the person had left and Aunt Karen hadn't noticed.

"Senor Joseph, he must go to Bethlehem for the taxes," Inez said.

"Everybody knows this part," Mora said, curling her fingers into commas. "Mary goes with on the donkey and she goes into labor and they didn't make a reservation at a hotel so she has the baby in somebody's barn."

That was pretty much the way Lucy remembered it, too. But Inez was shaking her head.

"It is tender, this story," she said.

"What's tender about giving birth on a pile of hay?"

"Is it because it was God's baby?" Lucy said.

"*Si*. And Senorita Mary, she knows this. She wrap the baby Jesus all up in—"

"Swaddling clothes," Mora said. "What is that, anyway? I mean, does anybody swaddle anymore?"

"They are perhaps rags hanging to dry."

"Mary didn't think to bring baby clothes? I don't get that, I mean, she must have been way pregnant."

"So she wrapped him up," Lucy said impatiently.

"With the tender care," Inez said. She touched the Bible page as if it were the Baby Jesus' skin. "You can imagine such a moment?"

She put her finger up to Mora, who was probably about to say something like, "Uh, no. Hello. I'm twelve!"

Lucy tried. She had no idea what it was like to be a mom, period, much less the mother of God's own kid. The only thing she could imagine was being scared to death. If Mary wasn't a whole lot older than her and Mora, she was still a kid herself. As far as Lucy was concerned, that was way too much responsibility.

"Now," Inez said, "nearby are the shepherds. They watch the

flocks of sheeps, and the angel comes to them and says the baby is born who will bring the peace to the earth. And more angels are there and they sing the beautiful song."

"Wait," Lucy said.

Inez looked up from her Bible.

"Did you say peace on earth? Like no wars and no fighting?"

Inez nodded.

"What happened to that?" Lucy said.

"What do you mean, what happened?" Mora lifted her palms. "The shepherds came, the wise guys came, we have Christmas."

"If there's supposed to be peace on earth, then how come people hate you for no reason and treat other people like dirt and kill people in wars? Like my mom?"

"What is going on in here?"

Aunt Karen darted into the kitchen, licking her lips and looking like she was trying to decide who to glare at first.

"We're having a discussion," Mora said.

"A discussion? Lucy looks like she's about to cry. Lucy, are you crying?"

"No," Lucy said, because she wasn't. She was just asking a question.

"No, your face is all red. Whatever this is, it's too upsetting for you right now." She moved to the table and bent over them like a praying mantis. "And you're making Mrs. Cluck very nervous."

"Mrs. Cluck!"

"Shhhh! I had enough trouble convincing her to come over for coffee. Inez, by the way, we need more cream in there." She waved her shiny fingernails over Inez's head and leaned closer to Lucy. "The poor woman has been through enough—she doesn't need to hear more drama in this house. Inez, I think you should stop for today."

"Mrs. Cluck is *here?*" Lucy whispered.

"Who's Mrs. Cluck?" Mora said.

"J.J and Januarie's mom."

"Their last name is 'Cluck'? I bet they get *so* teased about that."

"You two need to take this conversation elsewhere," Aunt Karen said. She straightened. "Inez, did you get more cream?"

Inez was already holding a small pitcher out to her.

"Just go put it on the tray. Never mind, I'll take it."

Aunt Karen licked her lips yet again and pulled her fingers like a rake through her hair and sailed back into the living room. Inez started to close her Bible, but Lucy shook her head.

"I want to hear the rest," she said.

Inez looked over Lucy's head to the doorway.

"She didn't say we *had* to stop," Mora said. "She said she *thought* we should. You have to admit there's a difference, Abuela."

"Please?" Lucy said. For some reason, she felt a little desperate, like this story could tell her something she needed to know. "How come the angels came to shepherds? If they wanted people to know about Jesus being God's son, why didn't they tell, like, I don't know, a newspaper?"

The peace slid back over Inez's face. "The angels are from heaven, and when they come, they connect—" She folded her fingers together—"They connect the people to what happens in heaven all the time—the singing and the peace. And they choose the shepherds because they have the job that is *monotonia*—how do you say?"

"Boring," Mora said.

"*Si.* This tells us, even when we are boring and we have no *importancia*, we can connect with the heaven."

"I haven't seen any angels," Lucy said, "and I've been looking."

"Seriously?" Mora said.

"We see the angels when we pray," Inez said. "They come to us, only they are different."

"No!" Lucy said. "I want the halos and the big fluffy wings."

Mora pulled in her chin. "Okay, that is just weird, Lucy."

"I know," Lucy said. "I'm the Class Weirdo. I'm living up to my title." She turned to Inez. "So, then what?"

"The shepherds go see the baby and that's why boys wear bathrobes in the Christmas play." It was easy to see how Mora knew what bored was. Her voice was going there.

Inez shook her head. "What is next, that is what is important."

"What?" Lucy said.

"The shepherds, they go and they tell everyone this message."

"Did anybody actually believe them?" Mora said.

Inez shrugged. "But this does not matter. It is important only that they tell what they see and what they know."

She looked right at Lucy, and Lucy felt a chill.

"And what about Senorita Mary?" Mora said.

"The Senorita, she treasures all these things and she thinks deeply because she is mama."

"She just sat around and thought?" Mora said. "I would totally be out getting some clothes for that baby."

Lucy tuned her out. Maybe that was what *her* 'mama' did when she started the Book of Lists. Maybe she was like Lucy and she had a hard time just sitting and thinking so she had to write things down. Dad told her Mom planned to write in it things she wanted Lucy to know about being a woman.

"Inez, I *told* you this was too upsetting for her right now."

Lucy looked up at Aunt Karen and realized through the blur that she was starting to cry. She brushed off the tears and headed toward her room and almost ran into a ball of a lady who stood between her and the hall. For a long minute she didn't recognize J.J.'s mom.

"Um, hi," Lucy said.

Mrs. Cluck's moon-shaped face didn't move at all. It didn't have to, because her body did the talking for her. A hunched-down neck and hands fretting and fidgeting at her waist announced that she was afraid of her very self.

"I'm going to walk Anita home," Aunt Karen said. "Shouldn't you be getting to soccer practice, Lucy?"

Lucy nodded, but even after Aunt Karen left with J.J.'s mother, she stood staring at the door.

"Okay, you're acting weird again," Mora said from the table. "Don't tell me—you saw an angel."

No, she hadn't seen an angel. But she'd gotten a message. Being scared of yourself was what living with meanness did to you.

She didn't know what to do with that, but somehow, it must be important. The knot in her stomach was cinching in.

Friday finally came, and as soon as Lucy came in from her run with Aunt Karen, she took a shower and put on her Los Suenos Dreams t-shirt. The whole team had promised to wear theirs—even Veronica, although she whined that it wasn't cute.

That turned out to be the least of anybody's worries. Ricky and Wolf-Man took every opportunity to hiss to J.J. that he was a sissy for wearing a shirt like the girls. Never mind that Gabe, Oscar, and Emanuel all had them, too.

The Queen B's wrote Lucy a Third Warning, telling her she was now sharing Class Weirdo status with her whole team. Especially J.J.

Nina and Skye just laughed every time they looked at any of the Dreams. Which was the entire morning.

By the time sixth period came, Veronica had changed out of her shirt into one of the extra outfits she kept in her fashion boutique of a locker, and Dusty had run out of "That's okay—we're awesomes." Even Gabe had put a sweatshirt on over his shirt, although he assured Lucy it was just because it was always cold in the Colonel's room.

The Colonel himself wasn't there when the bell rang to start class, but most of the kids got out their homework and kept a wary eye on the door. Lucy went to sharpen her pencil, just to be ready when he came in. When she turned around to go back to her seat, Wolf-Man was sitting on her desk. She shuddered. There was nothing worse than having a lizard on your homework.

"Do you mind?" she said.

"No," he said. He pointed to her shirt. "I wouldn't be advertising that."

"What?"

"That you play for a loser team."

"Actually, I don't," Lucy said. But she didn't feel good about saying it. She mostly wanted him to hush up. And get off her desk.

"Yeah, you do," Wolf-Man said. "Because look over there." He jerked his head toward J.J. "What does his shirt say, Rick?"

Ricky grabbed his desktop and leaned way out of his seat, craning his neck at J.J.'s chest. "Los Suenos Dreams," he said.

"Is that what it says?"

"That's what it says."

Wolf-Man shrugged at Lucy. "Then there you have it. If you're on the same team as the Half-Breed, you're on the loser team."

"Then so am I, dude." Gabe stood up and stripped off his sweatshirt. Somebody whistled.

"Me, too," Dusty said. She stood up as well.

"What about her?" Nina said, somehow spitting even though the question contained no s's. She jutted her square chin at Veronica, who was staring miserably at her desktop.

"She changed out of hers," one of the Queen B's piped up.

"I don't blame her," Skye said in her long-string voice. "I'd change, too, to keep from being a Half-Breed Lover."

Veronica's head came up, and her lip hung down. Tears trembled in her eyes. J.J. was clutching his desk so hard, even his wrists were white. Lucy lifted both hands over her head and let out a long, loud buzz.

Just in time for the Colonel to step into the room.

"Oops," Skye said—with a giant smile.

The class got itself to order, dropping into chairs and grasping at pencils and flipping open books. Only Gabe, Lucy, and Dusty were left standing.

But it was only Lucy who was summoned out into the hall. Visions of being dumped from the ODP tryout list—of Dad coming home from Albuquerque to bail her out of detention—of Aunt Karen saying this was just exactly what happened when you didn't act like a girl—it all flashed through Lucy's head as she leaned against the wall and waited for the Colonel to write her up. Send her to the office. End her life—even thought she wasn't the one playing dirty.

"Is there an explanation for you standing in the middle of my classroom making raucous noises?" the Colonel said.

"Yes, sir," Lucy said.

His eyebrows shot up to his tray of a hair-do. "And what might that be?"

Lucy opened her mouth to tell him that her best friend in the world was being attacked, and that soon he was going to break open and the Colonel was going to have a far worse scene on his hands than what he'd just witnessed. But it wouldn't come out. *Leave it—just leave it*, J.J. whispered in her head. And with his voice another light winked on. If she told—if anyone told—that would put him right in the middle, in the glare of attention, where he refused to be.

"Well?" the Colonel said.

Lucy tried to stand up taller. "Just a little pre-game rivalry," she said. "I guess it got out of hand."

"Rivalry."

"Between the Howl and the Dreams—soccer teams. We have a game tomorrow."

"I'm aware of that." The Colonel planted his hands on his hips. "I hope you conduct yourself on the field with more self-control than you just did in my classroom."

Lucy swallowed that and nodded.

"I don't think Ted Rooney would be very proud of that."

That one was harder, but Lucy nodded again.

The Colonel gave her one of his long looks, and then he nudged his head toward the door.

"That will be all," he said.

Lucy knew she should have broken into a sweat of relief. But as she hurried back to her seat, under the gazes of the Howl sneaked out over the tops of their math books, she only felt more knotted-up than ever.

12

In spite of the lack of banners and chocolate soccer balls and radio announcements, Game Day came anyway—crisp and cloudless without a trace of wind. Perfect soccer weather, Dad would say, even if there had been a monsoon going on. The thing Lucy missed the most as she put on her red, white, and blue Los Suenos Dreams uniform Saturday morning was Dad and his sandpapery voice outside the door saying, "You almost ready, Champ?"

"Ready, Dad," she whispered.

But she wasn't sure she was. On Thursday and Friday the team had worked hard again at practice, the way they used to, and Mr. Auggy made them repeat the rules about dealing with dirty playing about twenty more times. So it wasn't the Dreams that made her halfway wish somebody would cancel the day.

It was the rest of it, especially yesterday's scene in math class. She hadn't gotten into trouble, and the team all told her she was their hero. Except for J.J. The whole thing had only pushed him further away.

Dad was right. When it stopped being fun, something was wrong.

"Lucy—you better hustle, girl," Aunt Karen called from the kitchen. "I've got scrambled eggs ready for you. Let's move."

Oh, yeah. It had definitely stopped being fun.

Lucy managed to get down half the eggs, which Aunt Karen had tried to wrap in a tortilla the way Inez did except they all fell out the ends. It only made Lucy remember one more thing that made this feel like an un–Game Day: Inez wouldn't be in the stands, and Mora and her dance team wouldn't be out front with their pom-poms stirring the crowd to yell, "The Dreams don't die!"

What crowd?

When Emanuel and Dusty's moms pulled their vans full of team members up to the soccer field in Coyote Hills—which was only a little bit better than theirs used to be—the bleachers held a small knot of people, and Lucy didn't recognize any of them.

Veronica must have read Lucy's face because she said, "Don't worry. All our parents are coming."

Not mine, Lucy wanted to say, and missed Dad more than ever—until she saw J.J. swallow so hard his Adam's apple dipped and rose. His mother and father had never been to one of his games, and they probably never would.

"Your cheering section will be small but mighty, Team," Dusty's mom said. She smiled just like Dusty.

The Howl players were already warming up on the field. Their coach—a man who was skinny except for a belly that looked like he'd swallowed a watermelon—shooed them off so the visiting team could get on, and Lucy watched Ricky and Wolf-Man and the eighth grade boys saunter toward their bench with their soccer shorts hanging from their hips. Skye and Nina were right behind them, tilting their chins to acknowledge the Queen B's and a few others howling from the stands.

"They sound like a pack of coyotes," Oscar said through his toothpick.

"That's the point," Gabe said. "They're the Coyote Hills *Howl.* Get it?"

At least Gabe didn't call him a moron. They had to stick up for each other if they were going to get through this—because as the other four Howl players approached the bench, Skye and Nina and Ricky and even Wolf-Man stepped aside to let them through.

Lucy might have, too, if she were them. The two eighth grade girls were tall and muscle-hard and didn't look like they'd smiled since they were in kindergarten. Lucy would have bet the two boys were really twenty-year old men masquerading as kids that clucked at people.

"Guess what?" Carla Rosa said in a quavery voice.

"No guessing today, Miss Carla." Mr. Auggy gave the whole team a deep look. "You're a great team and you play a good, clean game. Let's send them a message that says that."

"The Dreams don't die, right?" Lucy said.

The answering "Right!" wasn't as enthusiastic as Lucy wanted, but at least nobody ran away.

When they'd finished the warm-up and Mr. Auggy gathered the team for his usual final pep talk before the game started, Veronica tugged Lucy's sleeve.

"Your aunt's here."

"Uh-huh," Lucy said. She was trying to focus on Mr. Auggy.

"Who's that lady with her?"

Inez?

Lucy's heart jumped at the thought and she squinted up into the bleachers. But the round, squeezed-tight woman next to Aunt Karen wasn't Inez. It was Mrs. Cluck.

She was wearing a pair of Aunt Karen's sunglasses, and Lucy was pretty sure the blue jacket she had on came out of her aunt's closet, too. Januarie sat on the other side of her, her round face shining like a happy moon, but Mrs. Cluck looked like a girl who'd been dragged to a birthday party where she didn't know anybody.

Januarie stood up—*on* the seat—and hollered, "J.J. lookit!"

J.J.'s head came up, and Lucy watched his mouth drop open before he quickly clamped it shut.

"You ready to play soccer?" the referee said.

It was a woman's voice. One Lucy knew only too well. She was sure before she whipped her head around that the ref was Ms. Pasqual.

She was all decked out like a professional official, complete with a black cap that barely contained her frizzy hair. She didn't look at all like a study hall teacher. In fact, she looked much more natural with a whistle in her mouth than she did in the classroom.

The attitude, however, was the same. "Well?" she said. "Are we going to play soccer or are we going to size each other up all day?"

Lucy shook herself loose and said, "The Dreams are ready."

Of course, as soon as Lucy stood in the center circle, facing one of the eighth grade girls who looked even bigger at close range, she forgot about Mrs. Cluck and Aunt Karen and who the ref was. She forgot everything except soccer.

When Ms. Pasqual blew the whistle, Lucy immediately passed the ball to Gabe, who was the most likely to keep it from the Howl until Lucy could get in position to see the field. Ricky was right on him, challenging Gabe with his eyes.

Exactly. Which meant he wasn't watching the ball. Gabe faked to the right and Ricky moved with him. Gabe was around him in a heartbeat, looking for an opening.

"To me!" Dusty cried.

Gabe's pass made it to her with no interference from the Howl. Lucy was amazed at how close Dusty got to the goal before Nina came in. When she stuck her foot out to snatch the ball, Lucy saw Dusty wince, but the ref didn't call a foul. Besides, Nina's pass went wild and Lucy trapped it and had the ball going back the other way before the Howl seemed to know what had happened.

Lucy had a straight shot to the goal so she set up to smack the ball with her instep. Suddenly there was another foot in there — one of the eighth graders — but he couldn't get any force behind the ball and Gabe captured it easily and took the shot.

Wolf-Man was playing goalie, and he barely got to his knee in time to make the catch. The sounds coming out of the Howls on the field were not happy ones. Their players might be big, but they didn't have the moves the Dreams had.

Lucy took a long, free breath and yelled, "Rebound, Dusty!"

Dusty nearly got the ball past Wolf-Man, who growled under his breath as he heaved it too hard from inside the box and put it right at J.J.'s eye level. He headed it to Veronica. Skye was all over her, and Lucy could see Veronica's lip wobbling. She tried to pass to Gabe, but the ball headed straight out of bounds.

Lucy raced after it, already planning how she was going to make the save, but then there was Ricky like he'd just jumped out of a closet, planting his body between her and the ball. His face was Halloween scary.

Lucy couldn't help plowing into him as the ball rolled away and the whistle blew.

"Don't give 'em a chance to set up, Ricky!" somebody yelled. "Throw-in!"

Ricky was already over the touchline, picking up the ball, when Ms. Pasqual blew her whistle again. Lucy froze. That never happened.

"That wasn't out of bounds, Ricky," she said. "That was a foul."

"Yeah!" Ricky said as he pointed at Lucy. "She charged me!"

"No, Einstein, you obstructed her. You can hurt somebody that way. Indirect kick."

"Naw, man, that's garbage!" some other player yelled.

"Come on, no way!" somebody else chimed in.

Coach Watermelon Belly obviously hadn't told them the 'don't scream at the official' rule. Or any other rule, as far as Lucy could see. So far, Dusty had been kicked, she herself had been obstructed, and Ms. Pasqual was reaching in her pocket like she was going for a yellow card. And they'd only been playing for five minutes.

"Is your team ready to kick, Rooney?" she said to Lucy.

Lucy nodded and signaled to Gabe. She would tap the ball and he would follow behind and shoot it. The Howl was still so busy protesting their foul, they didn't get it together to make a wall. Wolf-Man had to throw himself on Gabe's ball to keep it from going in. Which meant he used almost all of his six seconds getting the ball back into play. If the ref had called that, it would have meant another indirect kick for the Dreams, and Lucy was sure there would be a brawl if that happened.

The entire first half played that way. The Dreams kept possession of the ball most of the time and had a few near misses at the goal. The Howl never came close to scoring and broke the offside rule so many times it seemed like all the Dreams did was make indirect kicks. Although the Howl figured out fast that they had to make a wall and kept the Dreams from scoring, they were still hurling black looks and muttering between their teeth when Ms. Pasqual called time. Ricky turned his head toward J.J. and spit on the ground.

"Are you *looking* to be carded, son?" Ms. Pasqual said to him.

Coach Watermelon Belly pulled Ricky away before he could answer.

"How's it going out there?" Mr. Auggy said when the team was clustered around him. Everyone was red-faced and winded.

"They're not walkin' over us like they said they would," Gabe said.

"You're playing like a dream," Mr. Auggy said. "You're keeping it clean."

"They aren't."

All heads swiveled to Emanuel, who had actually spoken.

"Talk to me," Mr. Auggy said to him.

"One guy grabbed my shorts right here—" Emanuel yanked at his waistband—"and pulled me back when I was running down the field."

"I seen that!" Oscar said.

"And guess what?" Carla Rosa said, "that one girl that looks like Big Bird—she pulled my pants and I thought she was pulling them off and I had to stop and look and then she got the ball."

"She means Skye," Dusty said.

"Those are all things the ref doesn't see," Mr. Auggy said, "because she's the only official out there and she's running a short line."

Lucy didn't know what that was, but he seemed to be talking almost as much to himself as he was to them, like he was still figuring out what to tell them. He looked at Lucy. "Captain, do you want to talk to the ref? You have the right to question this."

"Should I?" Lucy said.

"Come on, we can handle it," Gabe said. "This is nothin'. I was expecting a lot worse."

Most of the team nodded or shrugged. Only J.J. stayed still.

Lucy wanted to ask him if anybody had messed with him on the field, but the words stopped in her throat.

"So does anybody *want* me to talk to the ref?" she said instead.

Nobody answered. J.J. wiped his face with his whole forearm. She couldn't see his eyes.

"All right, then," Mr. Auggy said, "so in the second half—"

"Is everybody staying hydrated?"

It was Aunt Karen with an insulated bag hanging from her shoulder and a soccer mom smile on her face.

"I think we're good, Miss Crosslin," Mr. Auggy said, nodding at the cooler on the bench. "I brought water."

"This kind has electrolytes in it," Aunt Karen said, and stuck a big enough bottle to hydrate all of Otero County into J.J.'s hand. "Did you see your mom up there?"

J.J. nodded and retreated to the bench.

"Who's not wearing sunscreen?" Aunt Karen said.

"I'm going to use the restroom, Mr. Auggy," Lucy said, and fled.

She might absolutely die if she had to watch Aunt Karen try to slather lotion on Oscar.

Or she might die right there in the restroom, because when she stepped inside, Skye appeared right behind her. Her eyes met Lucy's in the mirror over the sink and narrowed down into hyphens that would have made Mrs. Huntington proud.

Lucy tried to get into the stall without looking like she was trying to escape, but Skye wedged herself between Lucy and the door with more speed than anything Lucy had seen her do on the field. This was clearly obstruction.

"We never finished what we started," Skye said. Up this close, Lucy could see that even her two front teeth were long.

"What did we start?" Lucy said.

"That day at the lockers, *and* on the steps that morning. You were ready to 'knock us down' both times and then the Colonel butted in. So—" Skye snapped her braid back with a jerk of her head. "When's that gonna start?"

"What?" Lucy said.

"Du-uh—you 'knocking us down.'"

Mr. Auggy's rules tangled in Lucy's head with Dad's, and the Colonel's warning was barking over all of it. Even Inez's voice wove through. What was she supposed to say that wouldn't get her flushed down the toilet she was trying to get to?

"Look, the Colonel's not gonna come down from the bleachers and bust into the girls' bathroom to rescue you," Skye said. "It's just you and me now."

Lucy just looked at her.

"Okay, so if you're not gonna talk I will." Skye seemed to pull her whole face down her long nose. "We went way easy on you in the first half because we wanted to see what Pasqual was gonna be like as a ref, and since she's basically blind—" She drew 'blind' out into "ba-li-ind," "you just need to watch your back now. Well, not *you*, but your—"

The other stall door slammed open, and the big eighth grade girl came out. Skye's already very-white face went even whiter as the girl pointed her eyes at Skye.

"You need to stop talking," the girl said.

"I wasn't going to tell her, Tara—"

"Stop talking."

"I—"

The girl—Tara—thrust out her hand and closed her fingers together right in front of Skye's lips. "I said stop." She looked at Lucy, and, to Lucy's surprise, she smiled. "She's a seventh grader. You know you can't believe a thing they say."

"I'm a seventh grader," Lucy said.

"No you are not." Tara smiled harder, but it didn't reach her eyes. "I thought you were a much older woman. Look—what's your name?"

"Lucy," Skye said.

Tara did the fingers thing at her again. "Lucy, listen, forget what Skye just said to you—Hector's our captain and his orders come down to her through me. You totally get that, being a team captain yourself." She gave Lucy a knowing look, as if surely she understood the pressures of having so much authority. "We should probably get back out there."

"No," Lucy said. "I came in here to go to the bathroom. And I want to know how come she said somebody on my team needs to watch their back."

"Because she likes to act like she's important," Tara said. She directed a death stare at Skye, who seemed to have shrunk several inches. "I'm serious. Forget about it."

From the shove Tara then gave Skye toward the exit, Lucy was pretty certain *she* wasn't going to forget it. Lucy wasn't going to either. It was all she could think about as she finished up in the restroom and hurried back out to the field. She didn't care how mad he got at her, she had to warn J.J.

Because she had no doubt Skye was talking about him, and that she was telling the truth.

13

When Lucy got back to the field, Ms. Pasqual was already in the center circle, and even the frizz sticking out of the back of her ball cap looked impatient. The man-boy who must be Hector was there for the kick-off this time, not Tara. Even as Lucy nodded to the voices calling, "Let's go, Captain!" and, "It's about time, Lucy Goosey!" she scanned the players to find her.

Tara was on the Howl's end of the field, having an out-of-the-side-of-the-mouth conversation with Nina, who pointed her eyes at Skye. Before Lucy even got to the circle, Tara was doing the same thing with the other eighth grade girl, who also glared at Skye and did a quick side-step to the big kid with hair sticking up out of the top of his uniform.

So Lucy was right. They *were* planning something, and Tara was letting them all know that Skye had blabbed to one of the Dreams. Except that Lucy had no time to warn her team, which she couldn't do anyway. She would follow Mr. Auggy's rule and talk to the ref.

And tell her what? Frizzy Lady already had the whistle halfway to her mouth because Lucy was delaying the game. She sure wasn't going to believe something Lucy *almost* heard off the field, in the restroom, which the Howl would all deny anyway.

"Can I interest you in some soccer, Rooney?" Ms. Pasqual said.

"Sorry," Lucy said.

The instant she took her place, the whistle tooted and Hector had the ball out of the circle and off to the right side. Interesting choice to go that way instead of down the field toward the Dreams' goal. Especially since J.J. was there, wide open.

With the quickness he was getting so good at, J.J. directed the ball on first touch and headed the other way. Hector ran out in front of him, as if he were leading him straight for the goal. Lucy took in the field to see who could set up for a pass. Gabe was right in position, and Emanuel was behind J.J., ready if Hector managed to capture the ball and dribble his way.

Just as she looked back at J.J., he ran smack into Hector's back. Hector did a somersault, which J.J. maneuvered around without missing a step, but Ms. Pasqual blew long and hard on the whistle.

Another obstruction foul. When was the Howl going to get it?

"You can't bowl people out of the way, Cluck," Frizzy Lady said. "Indirect kick for the Howl."

What?

But Lucy called out, "Mark up!" and raced toward the other end of the field. Carla Rosa was waiting for her, instead of getting into position to stay on Nina, the wing forward.

"Guess what, Lucy?" she said. "That boy stopped right in front of J.J."

"I saw it, too," Emanuel said on her other side.

"The ref didn't," Lucy said. "Just stay on your attacker, okay? It'll be all right."

She did manage to block Hairy Chest's shot and do a 360 degree turn to get him off her. She passed the ball to Carla Rosa and ran up to take it back, just like they'd practiced. As she dribbled past the center line, she saw Dusty with no one on her—and felt a tug at her waistband. Tara was running beside her, body blocking the view from Ms. Pasqual.

"I'm not falling for it," Lucy said, and kept her eyes on the ball.

But she couldn't help slowing down as her shorts were yanked down over her hipbone. It was enough for Tara to snag the ball and she did. But she didn't take off down the field, with only poor Carla Rosa between her and the goal. She could have surprised Oscar in the goal. Instead, Tara passed the ball straight across to the other side where once again J.J. was clear. It was as if they were passing it to him on purpose.

Lucy gasped out loud. That was exactly what they were doing. Before the thought even took hold, J.J. had the ball and was dribbling in a nice zigzag pattern that had Ricky, Hector and Nina on the run. Although Lucy called out, "J.J.—man on!" to let him know they were behind him, she could see they weren't moving very fast. They were letting him drive unchallenged to the goal. And Wolf-Man wasn't moving up to cut down J.J.'s chances of shooting it past him on either side. Something was up—and there was nothing Lucy could do about it.

Suddenly it was as if Wolf-Man woke up, only Lucy knew he hadn't been sleeping. He rushed forward just as J.J. took his shot to the left. His clean follow-through gave Wolf-Man's side an airy brush—but he went down as if he'd been clubbed with a baseball bat.

"Oh, nuh-*uh*!" Lucy said.

She marched straight to Ms. Pasqual, who was blowing her whistle so hard the veins in her forehead were bulging like blue yarn.

"Careful Captain," she heard Mr. Auggy call to her.

Lucy nodded and took deep breaths, but her heart slammed with every hard, angry step.

"That was a clear case of challenging the keeper!" Hector was yelling, as if Ms. Pasqual weren't standing right next to him, watching Wolf-Man make a performance out of getting up off the ground. When he was on his feet, the crowd cheered and he waved bravely to them.

"I'm gonna throw up," Lucy heard Dusty mutter.

"May I ask a question?" Lucy said. "As Captain of my team?"

Ms. Pasqual looked at her twice, as if she didn't recognize her the first time. "What is it, Rooney?"

"Are you going to call that a foul? Because from back there, it looked like J.J. barely touched him, and he couldn't help doing it."

"That what it looked like to you?"

"Yes, ma'am," Lucy said.

"He tried to knock me over on purpose!" Wolf-Man said.

"He's been doing it all day—they both have." Hector waved what Lucy figured out was an invisible card. "He needs to be sent off."

Ms. Pasqual put up her hand. "This is the second time I've had to blow the whistle on you today, Cluck. But it's questionable."

"Hello!" Skye said. "It was so obvious!"

If she was trying to get back into her team's good graces, it wasn't working. Tara gave her the fingers-together-shut-up sign.

"It was not obvious to me and I'm the only one who counts." Ms. Pasqual patted the pocket where she kept the cards. "These stay here. The goal doesn't stand. The Howl throws in."

"Not fair!" Hector shouted—practically in her face.

Ms. Pasqual held up an invisible card, and he stomped off.

"Who's throwing in? Let's get this game under control."

That was exactly what Lucy intended to do. Heart still pounding out all the things she *so* wanted to shout into *Hector's* face, and the rest of the Howl as well, Lucy took her position at center field. But as soon as Hector threw the ball in, too hard, at Nina's feet, Lucy was on her, even though in the mark-up Nina belonged to Emanuel.

"Play back," Lucy told him, and when Nina alerted Lucy by faking only with her legs, Lucy took the ball easily and looked for J.J.

"Play up!' she called to him. "Cross!"

"Dude, Lucy Goosey!" Gabe shouted to her.

But Lucy ignored him and the fact that she should have been passing the ball to him, and, dribbling just a step ahead of a fire-breathing Skye, she turned in toward the goal and sent a high lofted pass to J.J.—who was waiting at the goal line. The ball came down just where J.J. could put his forehead on it and redirect it right into the goal. Just the way they'd done it a hundred times.

The tiny crowd from Los Suenos was on its feet, cheering as if the Dreams had just beaten Argentina. They didn't know that Lucy had played out of her position and called J.J. out of his. They didn't realize she'd cut Gabe or Dusty out of a chance to score the only goal that was going on the record today. They just knew the team had won.

As far as Lucy was concerned, J.J. had won, and even with the CHKs howling their protests, that was all she cared about.

"Another victory for the Dreams," Dad said on the phone as Lucy sat with it on the front porch. He laughed his sand-in-a-bucket laugh, and Lucy could almost see him smiling sunlight. She hoped he couldn't tell that she wasn't.

"We're all going down to Pasco's to celebrate in a few minutes," Lucy said. "As soon as Aunt Karen gets through emailing somebody."

"But you're not in a celebrating mood. What's going on, Champ?"

Lucy suddenly wanted to cry. Dad didn't have to see to tell exactly what she was feeling. He didn't even have to be here. She just wished so much that he was.

"Luce?" he said.

"It wasn't fun, Dad!" she blurted out.

"Ah."

"I played mad, and I never played mad before."

"You always play happy, don't you?"

"So does that mean there's something wrong?"

"I don't know what it means," Dad said. "Except that if you feel this bad about it, it's worth thinking about." She heard his voice thicken. "I'm sorry I'm not there to help you."

"Me, too."

"Only twenty-six more days."

Lucy did cry then, a little bit, because Dad was counting, too.

Across the street, she could see J.J.'s silhouette as he hopped over the low fence around his now-clean yard and headed down the street toward Pasco's. Lucy smacked away her tears.

"I'm proud of you, Champ," Dad said. "You go have fun. We'll get this figured out. Don't forget to pray."

"Okay."

"Take care of what I love."

Lucy didn't answer. She was sure she'd start crying again if she did. She'd only just hung up when the front door opened.

"Come read what I wrote," Aunt Karen said.

"Why?" Lucy said.

"Because it's about you." Aunt Karen pulled her through the door. "And I think it will cheer you up — although I don't know why you're all depressed. You scored big time."

"It was just a local game," Lucy said as she followed her aunt to the kitchen.

"It's all in how you pitch it, which is what I do for a living."

"You pitch?" Lucy said.

Aunt Karen pulled out a chair at the table in front of her laptop and motioned for Lucy to sit. "I make people think something is a very good idea. Read."

A letter appeared on the screen.

Dear Fred,

Lucy's game today was spectacular. Against tremendous odds — playing against a team with older, bigger, more experienced players — Lucy once again proved herself to be an exceptional player. She was the only team member to execute a goal, and in the final seconds of the game. She knows how to please a crowd —

"I didn't score the goal," Lucy said.

"I didn't say you did. I said you executed it, which is true. If you hadn't set it all up, it wouldn't have happened."

"Why didn't you mention J.J.?"

"Because he isn't trying out for ODP."

"I don't get it. Who's Fred?"

"You have a mind like a steel trap, Lucy." Aunt Karen leaned over and clicked something and the letter disappeared. "Fred Yancey. Our ODP contact."

"What if he thinks I'm bragging?" Lucy said. "You can't send that to him."

"I just did. It's how these things are done." She pulled the elastic off of Lucy's braid and pushed her fingers through her hair. "You take care of the playing and Mr. Auggy will take care of the coaching and I will take care of the politics."

Lucy pulled her head away and wriggled out of the chair. "Why can't you just —"

"Just what?"

"Just nothing." Lucy grabbed the elastic off the table and shoved her hair into a ponytail as she went for the back door. "I'm going to Pasco's."

The party was already happening when Lucy arrived, out of breath from running up Granada Street, saying, "Stay out of my life, stay out of my life," over and over. Claudia had watched her from the front of the House of Flowers 'n' Candy like Lucy was crazy, but at least Lucy hadn't shouted it into Aunt Karen's face like she wanted to. That Fred person was going to think she was pushy and conceited and everything they didn't want you to be for ODP. By the time Lucy sat herself down at a table with Dusty and Veronica, she was sure she had dragon-smoke coming out of her nose.

"Are you okay?" Dusty said.

"Uh, hello—she's so not!" Veronica said.

But Felix Pasco's microphone was squealing—though no one could ever figure out why Felix needed an amplifying system in his tiny café—and he was calling for their attention. As he began his usual speech about how proud he was of the Los Suenos Dreams, Carla Rosa leaned across the table and said to Lucy, "Guess what? I think Mr. Auggy is mad at you."

"Once again, our young people have proven that this town has a reason to come together—to forget our petty differences—"

Lucy looked around and found Mr. Auggy at the next table. He was looking up at Felix on the platform, but his eyes weren't listening. The small smile was very far away.

"What makes you think he's mad at Lucy?" Dusty whispered.

"Cause guess what, he just went like this at her."

Carla Rosa pinched in her eyebrows and scrunched up her mouth and looked absolutely nothing like Mr. Auggy. But when Lucy glanced at him again, she knew what Carla meant. It wasn't a mad look, though. It was a disappointed one, and that was worse.

Lucy tried to look away, but Mr. Auggy hooked her with his eyes and nodded toward the tables in the back where the old men sat to play checkers. Stomach knotting, Lucy followed him there. While half-hearted cheers punctuated Felix's on-and-on speech, Mr. Auggy sat across from Lucy and pushed back his shiny shock of hair. She had never seen him do that before.

"I know I played out of my position," Lucy said. "But I had to. They were making J.J. foul and he was going to get sent off and it wasn't fair."

"What if it had been Gabe?" Mr. Auggy said.

"Gabe would stand up for himself. J.J. won't because he's afraid he'll get in trouble and Winnie the State Lady will put him in foster care—even though she probably won't, only he doesn't think that—"

Mr. Auggy looked like he was going to say one thing, and then he shook his head and said another. "So it was personal."

"What does that mean?"

"It wasn't really about soccer. It was about taking care of J.J."

"It was kind of both," Lucy said. "J.J. doesn't want me, like, protecting him at school, but I can on the field and he doesn't know I'm doing it."

"J.J. knows exactly what you're doing, Lucy."

He didn't call her 'Captain,' or 'Miss Lucy', and he was talking in the voice he used when he and Dad were discussing serious things.

"Here's the deal," he said. "It can't be both soccer and personal. You don't work out your problems with your friends or your enemies on the field. They have to be separate, or you won't make it."

"I'm sorry," Lucy said.

Mr. Auggy nodded, and the small smile twitched at the corners of his mouth. Lucy had never been so happy to see it.

"This could be the part where you start to want to rip out my nose hairs," he said.

"Not yet," Lucy said. "Um, Mr. Auggy?"

"Yeah, Captain."

"Could I ask you a question? It's not about soccer."

He nodded her on.

"Is it true that boys—well, men, too—don't like girls acting like they're stronger and smarter, even when they are?"

"I need more information to answer that," Mr. Auggy said, like he was picking his words one by one.

"Well, like, do girls always have to make guys think everything is their idea to get anything to change?"

She could see something dancing in Mr. Auggy's eyes, but he didn't laugh at her, so at least there was that.

He cleared his throat. "Here's how I look at it. I'm just one guy, but I think I speak for a lot of us when I say that nobody, girl or boy, should have to be anything other than who they really are just to make somebody else feel better about themselves."

Lucy sorted that through. "Okay—so, then, why isn't it okay for me to stand up for J.J. when he's being bullied, just because I'm a girl?"

Mr. Auggy's eyes stopped dancing. "It isn't just because you're a girl. It's because J.J. has to learn to stand up for himself."

"But if he gets into a fight, they'll put him in foster care!"

"Who said anything about fighting?" Mr. Auggy said. "That isn't the only way J.J. could take on the bullies, but it's the only way he knows. He doesn't feel comfortable yet using any of the other means available to him."

"I'm available to him."

Mr. Auggy shook his head. "You aren't a means, Lucy. You're a friend. That's what he needs."

Lucy folded her arms. She was about to say, 'Am I just supposed to stand by and watch them cluck at him in front of the whole school?'

But the door jangled open and Aunt Karen swept in. Now, *there* was somebody whose nose hairs Lucy would gladly have pulled out.

As Aunt Karen hurried toward the Dreams' table, Lucy stood up. There was no telling what she'd say to them about how Lucy had 'executed the goal.'

"I better get back," Lucy said.

Mr. Auggy smiled his small smile. "I hope that helped."

"I'll let you know," Lucy said.

14

By third period on Monday, it looked to Lucy like the CHKs were going to leave the Dreams alone now that the game was over.

No note from the Queen B's appeared on her desk, assuring her that she still held the Class Weirdo title after her three warnings. Ricky and Wolf-Man didn't call J.J a Half-Breed and the eighth graders didn't cluck at him in the hall. Even Skye and Nina left their cell phones in their purses—though Lucy did notice that Nina walked a few steps ahead of Skye in the hall on the way to science class.

Maybe Mr. Auggy was wrong. Maybe personal problems did get solved on the soccer field.

Or not.

While Mrs. Marks stood with her back to them at the chalk board and droned, bee-like, about the parts of the cell she was drawing, the CHKs woke up—and they had apparently not had good dreams. The tension stiffened in the room just from the way they sat up in their desks and tapped their pens and breathed through their nostrils until Lucy could almost hear it over Mrs. Marks' nucleus and protoplasm lecture.

No one said a word. No one had to. The hate hung in the air as if Dusty and Veronica's moms had painted it on a banner that hung directly over J.J.'s head.

As soon as she got to study hall, Lucy started a new list:

DEAR GOD, WHY DO THE CHKS DESPISE J.J.? WHY?

1. Because he's part Native American and part white? Who cares? Everybody in New Mexico is half something and half something else, except us bo'lillos. Most of THEM are half and half. That can't be it.

2. Because his Dad had to go to jail for a while for being mean? No way. Gabe says his dad says half the people in Coyote Hills have been in his jail some time. I kind of wish they all were right now.

Lucy looked up to make sure nobody was reading over her shoulder. Only Ms. Pasqual was watching her, and when Lucy caught her eye, she nodded toward the door. Lucy made her way through the thickening tension and followed her out into the hall, this time taking her list with her.

Ms. Pasqual did her usual arm fold and just looked at Lucy for a minute. A long minute. Until Lucy wanted to yell, *What?*

"I can't figure you out, Rooney," she said finally.

What was Lucy supposed to say to that?

"You don't follow the trends. You don't giggle. You don't live for whatever pops up next on that little screen."

"What little screen?" Lucy said.

"Exactly. You play soccer like a young Brandi Chastain, with probably more character, and you sit in my study hall and pray. Who are you really?"

"Excuse me?"

"You're a thirty-five year old woman in a twelve-year-old body, aren't you?"

Lucy started to shake her head, until she saw something cross Ms. Pasqual's face that lit it up and turned it into sunlight. Just like Dad's when he smiled.

"I didn't bring you out here to give you grief, Rooney, although I do enjoy it. I just wanted to tell you I'm praying for you."

"Oh," Lucy said. Did Ms. Pasqual know about Dad being away? About ODP? About Aunt Karen pitching her like an idea? About Veronica and Gabe and J.J.? Could teachers find out about that stuff?

"You're trying so hard to behave with integrity in this mess of a world, and I'm just praying you can continue to do it."

"Thanks."

"If something ever goes down and tries to take you with it and you need somebody, I'm here."

Lucy could only stare.

"Don't worry, Rooney," Ms. Pasqual said. "I'll leave the whistle at home."

That afternoon at soccer practice, Mr. Auggy asked them how things went with the Howl at school that day.

"Weird," Gabe said.

"Weird how?"

"Weird like they want to take us all out and smack us around—"

"Ga-abe!" Veronica wailed.

"—but they know they can't and that makes it worse." He shrugged his big shoulders, which seemed to Lucy to have expanded in the last two weeks. "It was easier when they were calling us names and stuff."

Nobody disagreed.

"Well, then," Mr, Auggy said, "you have a serious decision to make."

"Guess what?" Carla Rosa said. "My dad says I don't make very good decisions."

"Guess what?" Oscar said to her.

"Look out now, Oscar," Mr. Auggy said. "Don't get yourself buzzed."

Oscar looked insulted. "What? I was just gonna say her old man don't know what he's talkin' about. She makes good decisions all the time. She's here, ain't she?"

"Well, ding, ding, ding, Oscar. I think."

"What's the decision?" Lucy said.

Mr. Auggy scrubbed at his face with his hand. "The Howl Coach called me. He and his team would like a rematch next Saturday. If we did agree, we'd play here."

"Here?" Gabe said.

"Guess what—"

Mr. Auggy put his hand up. "I know, the place still looks like a tornado went through it, but since your win Saturday, a couple people in town have come over from The Dark Side. Claudia, for one."

"Yes — chocolate soccer balls!" Veronica said.

"They're going to fix up the field?" Lucy said.

"They're going to try."

"Then we gotta play, don't we?" Gabe said.

Lucy had to stare at him. It wasn't just his shoulders and his voice that had changed. Back when the Dreams had first formed, Gabe acted like he was doing them all a favor just by showing up. Now here he was, taking the team as seriously as she did.

"They were pretty mean, though, Mr. Auggy," Dusty said. She already had one arm around Veronica and one around Carla Rosa, and Lucy knew she'd have put another one around her if she had an extra.

"I made their coach aware of that," Mr Auggy said. "And I intend to talk to the ref."

Veronica gave a nervous giggle. "Frizzy Lady?"

"I don't think she's that frizzy anymore," Lucy said.

"But it's entirely up to you."

Lucy knew Mr. Auggy meant the whole group, but his eyes rested on J.J.

J.J., who had barely said a word all day. She was missing him almost as much as she missed Dad, and he was right here. Somehow that felt even lonelier.

J.J. swallowed and unhunched his shoulders. For the first time ever, Lucy thought he looked a little like his mother.

"I'm in," he said.

But he still didn't meet Lucy's eyes.

"All right, J-Man!" Gabe said. "Let's really rock 'em this time."

"I do have one concern if you decide you want to do this," Mr. Auggy said. "And that is that they may want to use this rematch to settle some personal score. Anybody know what that's about?"

Everyone shook their heads, including Lucy. She'd been thinking about it all day, and she was no closer to an answer. She'd given up on angels showing up, or any other signs like Mary got. Lucy was even pondering, and so far, nothing.

"So what do you say?" Mr. Auggy held out his palm. "You want some time to think about it?"

They all looked at Lucy.

"Let's take a vote," she said.

It was unanimous.

But there was still a cloud of heaviness hanging over the upcoming game as the week went on, even as they watched the bleachers become whole again and the banners go up over Granada Street and Highway 54 and the chocolate soccer balls appear in Claudia's window display.

Even at ODP practice. Maybe more so there, because on Wednesday, Mr. Auggy announced that he'd received a date for the tryout in Albuquerque.

"Sunday, September 20th," he said.

Lucy felt her stomach twist. "That's so soon."

"It's the day after our game with the Howl," Dusty said. "That just makes me tired for you."

And then she plopped down on the ground, flung her face into arms folded over her knees, and cried.

Lucy sat beside her and tried to decide whether to hug her. She still wasn't very good at this.

"It's okay, Dusty," she said. "I can do it."

"But I can't!"

"You don't have to."

"No, I mean I can't do *this.*" She raised a tear-striped face. "These practices. I'm sorry, *Bolillo,* but it's just too hard for me."

Lucy looked at Mr. Auggy, and begged him with her eyes not to say she had to handle this because she was the Captain.

"Hey, Miss Dusty," he said as he squatted beside her. "Our agreement was anybody can stop anytime they want, no hard feelings. Right, Miss Lucy?"

"Right. Just be here to cheer me on, okay? You always do that so good—better than me."

"I do?" Dusty said.

"Yeah, you're so cheerful it's disgusting," Gabe said.

Mr. Auggy buzzed him, but there was a laugh in his voice.

The laugh disappeared again, though, as he walked with Lucy to the Jeep after an hour of practicing nothing but fakes. Lucy had done so many step-overs and shimmies and stops and starts she could hardly walk like a normal person.

Once again Mr. Auggy asked her if this was too much for her, too. Once again, Lucy told him no. With so many other things so mixed up and uneasy, like they always seemed to be, her soccer dream was the one thing that stayed the same. Maybe playing teams like the Howl wasn't part of that dream. ODP and beyond—that was.

But the mixed up, uneasy things dragged at her more and more, and she found herself on Thursday leaning toward home all day so she could have Bible study with Inez. Mary hadn't been all that helpful so far, but something pulled at Lucy, something that said the next part of her story might be.

"Ah, Senorita Mary," Inez said when the three of them were sitting at the table in front of a bowl of fruit.

She ran her finger down the onion-skin page like she always did, and Lucy felt herself sigh. Inez was like one of those oasis things in the middle of a desert of stupidness.

"The boy Jesus, he is now twelve years old," Inez said.

Mora looked up from the apple she was examining. "I wonder if he was—"

"Do *not* say 'hot'," Lucy said.

"—and Senora Mary and Senor Joseph—"

"I am so glad those two people finally got married."

"—they take the boy Jesus to Jerusalem for the feast. It is a very long walk."

"They walked?"

"What did you expect—a limo?" Lucy said.

"It takes many days, but when they arrive, it is good for the boy Jesus."

"Why?" Mora poked her finger out like a period. "Never mind—I know it wasn't because he met a cute girl."

"When the feast is over, the mama and the papa, they are walking

144

home with their friends—many travel together—and they wonder, where is the boy?"

"What—you mean they didn't make sure he was with them?" Mora said. "What is this, *Home Alone Four?*"

Lucy got up on one knee. She'd never heard this part. Maybe Reverend Servidio had preached about it, but that didn't mean she'd actually heard it.

"They are *frenetico*," Inez went on.

"Freaked out."

"And they return to Jerusalem to search for three days. Where do you think the boy Jesus is found?"

Lucy thought about it. A twelve year old boy, left behind? The twelve year old boys she knew would be looking for something to eat or somebody to punch and make weird noises with. But this was the son of God they were talking about . . .

"Was he in a church?" Lucy said.

Inez's eyes lit up like birthday candle flames. "*Si!* He is with the priests and the people of knowledge, and they are amaze at the questions he asks and the things he knows for a boy so young."

"So, did his parents punish him?" Mora said. "I mean, if I did that, you'd ground me 'til ninth grade."

Inez shook her head, eyes closed. "The boy Jesus, he says he does what he must do. He is in the house of his Father."

"God," Lucy said.

"*Si*. And Senora Mary, she thinks on these things and she raise the boy to obey—"

"Wait a minute." Mora had both hands making periods. "He was the Son of God, but he still had to obey his parents?"

Inez nodded. "He must become wise and tall to do what his Father have for him to do. He must learn to be the friend to God and people."

"He must learn not to ditch his parents and make them look for him for three days," Mora said.

"*Si.*"

"So what about Mary?" Lucy said.

Inez ran her finger down the page. "'They did not understand what he was saying to them,'" she read. "'But his mother treasured all these things in her heart.'"

"That's all she did was treasure," Mora said with a yawn. "She's not as interesting as some of those other Bible chicks we read about."

But Lucy was switching knees. "So that's why she didn't punish him. She didn't get him, but she was just letting him be him."

Inez made her face smooth. "Talk of this more."

Lucy squinted and saw a list in her head. "Okay, so, Number One, he knew what he was *going* to be and that's why he was hanging out with those smart church guys. But, Number Two, he wasn't old enough to be that yet so he had to grow up and get ready for it. And Number Three ..." She stared for a moment at her third finger, still curled into her palm. "His mom knew it was going to be big so she just watched and remembered everything." She looked at Inez. "Right?"

Mora dropped her chin into her hands, propped up by her elbows on the table. "Now you're going to make us figure out how we're like Mary and seriously, Abuela, I'm not a mother so I don't get it."

For once Lucy had to agree with Mora.

Inez closed the Bible and folded her hands on its cover. "Senora Mary," she said. "She knows God always, no matter how he comes. By angel. As baby. As the song in her heart." Inez pressed her hand to hers. "What she does not know of God, she will wait for. She will treasure." She looked straight at Lucy. "He will speak. This you cannot stop. You can only treasure."

Someone spoke just then—at the top of her shrill voice from down the hall—and it definitely wasn't God.

"That is *it*, you evil cat!" Aunt Karen shrieked. "You are going to the pound!"

Lucy bolted from the chair and heard it fall over behind her as she tore down the hall. Aunt Karen stood outside the guest room door, holding Lollipop straight out in front of her by the scruff of her neck. Lolli's belly wobbled as she kicked to be free.

"Put her down!" Lucy said.

"Oh, I'll put her down, all right!"

Aunt Karen shoved Lucy's door open with her foot and marched into the room with Lollipop still flailing in front of her.

"Where is it, cat?" She gave Lolli a shake. "Where is my tennis bracelet?"

"She can't tell you, Aunt Karen," Lucy said. "Put her down—please."

Aunt Karen dropped the kitty on the bed and threw open the lid to Lucy's toy chest. "Well, there's the earring I've been missing." She pulled out the gold hoop and held it between her fingers as if it were teeming with bacteria. "I know she took my tennis bracelet and it's in here someplace."

She used her leg to push Lucy's giant stuffed soccer ball aside and bent upside down to inspect under the bed.

"I haven't seen it," Lucy said.

"You didn't see my earring either but it was in here." She ran her hand along the windowsill.

Lucy actually *had* seen it, which made her guilty enough to say, "Okay, so I'll look for it. Aunt Karen, please stop going through my stuff."

"I'm looking for *my* stuff." Aunt Karen yanked the covers back on Lucy's bed and plucked up her pillow—and exposed the Book of Lists.

Aunt Karen stopped, pillow in hand. Lucy dove from the foot of the bed, but Aunt Karen grabbed the Book up and held it above Lucy's head.

"Is this it?" she said. "Is this my sister's book?"

And then she opened its green cover with the raised gold leaves and stared.

"You've written in it." She pointed her eyes at Lucy like an accusing finger. "You've written in it, and you've ruined it."

15

Lucy scrambled to her feet on the bed, snatched the Book of Lists out of Aunt Karen's hand, and leapt for the hallway. She didn't take the time to close the door behind her, but if she had, she would have slammed it. She was beyond eye-rolling, way past sighing and shrugging. And if she had to speak, it would be in worse than a get-out-of-my-face tone. All she wanted to do was run away and take her Book to a safe place.

But there was no going anywhere. Inez blocked the hall to the kitchen, with Mora peering over her shoulder. Aunt Karen was already behind Lucy. And at the other end, standing in front of the guest room, was Mrs. Cluck. Lucy was too panicked to even wonder what she was doing there.

Lucy tried to bowl her way to the kitchen, but Inez got her by the shoulders and turned her around. She put both arms around Lucy's chest and held her there. Lucy could feel her breathing hard.

"Give me that book," Aunt Karen said, doing some hard breathing of her own as she held out a pointy-nailed hand.

"It's mine."

"It's my sister's."

"She was going to write in it for me."

"And now you've scribbled in it and destroyed one of the only pieces of her we have left."

"Dad said I could do it," Lucy said.

"Your dad can't see your handwriting—or the stuff you've put in there." Aunt Karen grabbed again for the book, but Inez took a step backward and Lucy went with her.

"This book belong to Senorita Lucy," Inez said—in the quietest voice Lucy had *ever* heard her use. "Senor Ted said to me no one must ever touch it."

"Well Senor Ted isn't here, is he? Lucy, give me that book."

Inez pushed Lucy behind her and this time took a step forward, until she was mere inches from Aunt Karen. She had to look up at her, but she seemed tall and strong.

"You will not take this when I am in the house," Inez said.

"Lucy," Mora whispered behind her.

Lucy shook her head, but Mora put her lips close to Lucy's ear.

"Let me hide it."

When Lucy looked at Mora, she saw tears sparkling on her eyelashes.

Lucy nodded, and Mora slid the book from Lucy's hands and slipped out of the hall.

"Only Senor Ted can fire me," Inez was saying.

"Fire you!" Lucy threw herself in front of Inez. "You can't fire her!" she shouted at Aunt Karen. "You can't!"

"I just did. If I'm going to be in charge of you, I have to have people who are going to support me." Aunt Karen's eyes darted back to Inez. "You have five minutes. I'll write you a check for the rest of this week."

"I want no check," Inez said.

She turned, stiff as a broom, and went toward the kitchen.

"Inez, no!" Lucy said.

She started after her, but Inez looked back and shook her head.

"I will go before things are said that cannot be unsaid." Her dark eyes glinted over Aunt Karen.

"Four minutes," Aunt Karen said.

"What if she doesn't leave in four minutes?" Lucy said, and she cared nothing about tone. "Are you going to call the Sheriff?"

"No! No sheriff!"

Both Aunt Karen and Lucy whipped their heads toward the shuddering figure in the corner. Mrs. Cluck had both hands pressed so hard to her lips her fingertips went white. She shook her head, her shoulders, her knees and slid down the wall to the floor.

"Just—go someplace, Lucy," Aunt Karen said. "We'll finish this later."

She crouched beside J.J.'s mom, and Lucy tore for the kitchen. Inez was already going out the back door with Mora behind her.

"Inez, don't go!" Lucy said.

Mora shook her head at Lucy. "She's not even talking now, which means she's, like, triple mad." She backed toward the door herself, looking over her shoulder. "Your book's safe," she whispered. "We'll be back, I know we will."

Inez barked something in Spanish from the yard and Mora fled. Lucy stood staring at the door until it disappeared in a blur.

She had never, ever, felt so alone.

The crying grew quiet in the hall. Lucy grabbed her soccer ball and stormed out into the yard, choking back her own tears. Think. She had to think what to do. Because she had to do something.

She bent her leg and dropped the ball on her thigh, over and over, but it did no good. Neither did kicking it against the fence until Artemis Hamm fled from the yard, or dribbling around the Mexican elder tree and the tool shed and the patio table until she was heaving for air. When Aunt Karen appeared at the back door, Lucy was still sure anything that came of her mouth would make the get-out-of-my-face tone sound like a lullaby.

"So I suppose you've buried it or something," Aunt Karen said. She pulled her big, long sweater tight around her and held it with her folded arms as she came slowly down the steps and dropped into a patio chair. "Mrs. Cluck got upset when you started in about the sheriff. She's had too many bad experiences with that."

Lucy managed to say, "I'm sorry."

"She's a good woman," Aunt Karen said. "I'm trying to help her." She brushed a scattering of gold-coin leaves off the table. "I'm trying to help you, too, Lucy. I know you can't see that."

Lucy tucked her ball under her arm and went for the back door.

"We can't work this out unless we talk about it," Aunt Karen said.

"I can't talk about it to you," Lucy said from the top step.

"Come sit down."

Lucy let the screen door slap shut behind her. She had to talk to Dad, or she was going to say all those things she couldn't get rid of with a soccer ball.

But the phone on Dad's end rang and rang and rang. When his voice mail came on, she hung up. The sound of him hit the tender spot inside her and made it hurt.

She didn't try again that night because every time she ran into Aunt Karen, she started in about how they had to 'have a conversation about this thing.' Lucy stayed in her room, comforting Lollipop and wishing for her Book of Lists. Mora said it was safe, and Lucy knew she wouldn't read it, but not having it made God seem so far away.

Inez said God would speak. She just had to wait and treasure.

Lucy sat up. Inez didn't say you could only treasure one way—

Lucy gently deposited Lolli on the windowsill. Then she put her head under her pillow. It was worth a try.

"Number One," she whispered. "Inez understands. Dad understands. Even Ms. Pasqual understands. Why am I stuck with Aunt Karen? She doesn't know anything about me.

"Number Two. I was just starting to get Mary. How am I supposed to know if I'm right without Inez?

"Number Three. I'm trying to treasure, here, God, but if you're not going to answer me, can I at least talk to my Dad?"

Then she fell asleep, because there was no Number Four.

Number Three was still on her mind when Lucy woke up before the sun the next morning. She dumped all the change from the jar on her bookshelf into her backpack and after she made sure Lollipop was safe in the toy chest with the lid propped open, she shut her door and crept out the back without waking Aunt Karen up.

It was still too early for the team, and Lucy sat alone on the front steps of the school. The sun was rising over the Sacramento mountains into a cloudless sky, lighting the banner strung over Granada Street straight ahead of her, from Mr. Benitez's grocery to Felix Pasco's café.

PRIDE IN LOS SUENOS DAY
SATURDAY SEPTEMBER 20
DREAMS VS. HOWL 10:00 A.M.

it said in red and blue letters painted by Dusty and Veronica's moms.

Mr. Benitez and Felix Pasco were going to sell refreshments. Sheriff Navarra said the people who owed him community service for their misdemeanors, whatever that meant, would have the bleachers in shape for the fans. Claudia said she had mounds of candy soccer balls for the team for after the game.

Lucy put her face on her knees. She should have felt happy about all that—and about the ODP tryout on Sunday in Albuquerque—and about getting to see Dad there and telling him in person that so far her grades didn't stink and she kind of liked being the Class Weirdo. She wished so much that she could just treasure all that and forget about the rest.

"You're not crying, are you?"

Lucy brought her face up. J.J. stood at the bottom, scraping the sole of his shoe on a step.

Lucy didn't answer at first. They were the first words he'd spoken to her in so long, and they were stiff.

"Not yet," she said finally.

He shrugged his bony shoulders and climbed the rest of the steps like doing it was painful. As he leaned on the railing a few feet from her, Lucy could feel her heart pounding.

"You sad about Inez?" he said.

"You know about that?"

"My mom told me."

Lucy felt her eyes widen. "You and your mom talked?"

"Mr. Auggy says I gotta talk to her."

"Is it okay?"

"I guess."

"Well—that's good."

Lucy felt hope rising up in her. They were talking. Maybe it was all right now.

J.J. bounced the heel of his tennis shoe off the bottom of the railing. "He says I gotta talk to you, too."

His voice shot up at the end. Lucy's heart stopped pounding and began to sink.

"I don't want you talking if you don't want to," she said. "I hate it when somebody tries to make me talk."

J.J. frowned all the way down his long legs. "He says I gotta tell you why I got mad, or I'm gonna be like my dad."

Although Lucy's heart had sagged as far as it would go, she shook her head hard. "You could never be like your dad. He's like—like a grown up CHK. You're not like that—"

She stopped, because J.J. had straightened to a pole, and his jaw muscles were taut in the sides of his face.

"What?" Lucy said. "What did I say *now?*"

"You don't know," he said.

And then he climbed over the railing and dropped to the ground. She could hear his footsteps pounding away and she went to the railing and leaned down to crawl under it and go after him.

"Lucy Goosey!"

Lucy looked down to see Gabe coming up the steps, grinning like a chimpanzee.

"Not now, Gabe," she said.

"Not now what?" He tugged at her sleeve and made her sit. Then he eased down beside her and leaned back on the next step with his elbows. "You know you wanna talk to me."

"No, actually, I don't. I want to talk to J.J."

Gabe made a kissing sound that set the hairs on the back of her neck straight up.

"I said I wanted to talk to him, not kiss him!" she said. "I don't want to kiss any boy, including you."

That wasn't exactly making it seem like Gabe's idea, but it was what came out. Mora wouldn't be impressed.

"Bummer, dude," Gabe said, though he didn't look at all disappointed.

"But I wasn't tryin' to kiss you. I was tryin' to keep you from runnin' after the J-Man and makin' him feel like a loser."

"What?" Lucy said.

But even as the word came out of her mouth, she knew exactly what he meant. The same thing Mr. Auggy meant.

"That's what all the tickling me and stuff is about—keeping me away from J.J.?"

"Mostly," Gabe said. He wiggled his eyebrows. "And it made Veronica jealous. She was acting like she owned me."

"You disgust me," Lucy said.

"I know." Gabe sat up but he kept looking at Lucy.

"Now what?" she said.

"You gotta let the J-Man work this out himself."

"Why couldn't you just say that?"

"Because." He shrugged. "Girls like to think everything is their idea."

"Then you give me *your* idea," Lucy said, shoving him in the shoulder. "Are we supposed to just stand there and let the CHKs make him miserable?"

"No."

"Then what do we do?"

Gabe looked puzzled—not a look she'd seen often on his face. "You're the one who always figures that stuff out, Lucy Goosey. You'll come up with something."

"Gabe!" a girly voice yelled.

His eyes twinkled and he started to lean toward Lucy.

"Come near me and I'll tell her exactly what you're doing," Lucy said.

"Dude," he said. "You're turning into an actual girl."

Lucy was glad it was test day in all three morning classes so she didn't have to talk much to anybody. The only person she wanted to have a conversation with was Dad, and when everyone else headed for the cafeteria from the lockers after fourth period, Lucy pretended she'd forgotten something and promised to catch up.

"You're all stressed out about the game and the tryout, aren't you?"

Dusty said to her. "I know I'm supposed to cheer you up, but I've been trying all day and I don't think it's working."

"I'll be better after lunch," Lucy told her.

Once Dusty was gone and the halls were eerie-empty, Lucy poured all of her change from her backpack into the pocket of her sweatshirt and hurried around the corner. There was a payphone at the end of the eighth grade hall—

"Stop right there."

Lucy came to a halt and stuffed down a groan. Did the Colonel spend all his lunch periods waiting in the halls for her to break a rule?

"We didn't get clear on this last time?" the Colonel said.

She turned to face him and hoped she wouldn't cry. All she wanted was to talk to her dad.

"We did," Lucy said.

He shot up one eyebrow. "But you're still here. Why is that?"

Lucy suddenly wanted to slide down the wall like Mrs. Cluck. She was too tired for a step-over or a shimmy or any other kind of fake.

"I wanted to use the phone," she said.

"No phone calls during school hours," he said.

"I didn't know."

"Student handbook. Page five. Paragraph two." Something twinkled in the Colonel's eye and then winked away. "Too bad all the rules aren't in the handbook."

"Excuse me?"

"Like the one about not using soccer as a weapon of mass destruction."

Lucy couldn't stop her mouth from falling open, Veronica style.

"The Howl tried to force a send-off on J.J.," the Colonel said. "You saw that, but you let them get to you."

"You were there?" Lucy said. "At the game?"

"I never miss seeing the Howl play," the Colonel said. "It's the only way I can figure out what the kids from Coyote Hills are about."

He pushed his hands into his pockets like two shovels, as if he were settling in for a conversation. Lucy's mind chased itself. Skye had said something in the restroom about him being in the stands but she'd thought she was trying to be funny. He really was a Howl fan?

"I started the first Howl team," he said. "Way back—twenty years ago."

"Twenty?" Lucy couldn't help saying.

"Had a boy on my team, talented kid, so fast I thought at first he should be a forward. He was good, but not great—not until I saw his promise as a defender. And then, he started to shine."

The Colonel's eyes were shining, too, like there was more to this tale she should know. She stopped looking for an escape route.

"He could have gone pro, I think, except he couldn't control his temper. He'd have a problem with an official and kick the ball off the field. Blew up every time he was fouled."

"Was he Ricky's father?" Lucy said—and then hoped she wasn't using an attitude tone.

Both the Colonel's eyebrows shot up. "You have good instincts," he said.

Lucy didn't know about instincts. She'd just blurted it out.

"No, he wasn't Ricky's father," the Colonel said. "He was J.J.'s."

Lucy absolutely could not keep her mouth closed this time. "J.J.'s father played soccer?" she said.

"Unfortunately, not for long. He couldn't handle the discipline, didn't like being sent off every game for his temper." The Colonel squinted as if he were looking into that faded time. "If I could have kept him playing, he might not have gotten into all the trouble he did. Let's just say J.J.'s dad made a lot of enemies in Coyote Hills. He would never let anything go. When the kids teased him about his last name—and Cluck is an unfortunate one, I'll admit—he went after their pets. When somebody fouled him on the field and it didn't get called, he gave them a penalty himself, off the field. He's not welcome there any more, even after all these years."

Lucy felt like a flashlight had just turned on in her head. "Is that why the CHKs are so mean to J.J.? Because of his dad?"

"I don't think that was it in the beginning. I think they just saw somebody they could pick on—and then when they put it together with what their parents told them about his dad, that just made them feel justified." The Colonel rubbed the side of his face. "I don't want to go into too much detail, because I think it's better kept in the past, where the Howls don't seem to want to leave it. They're giving J.J. the penalties his dad gave their dads."

"But that doesn't make any sense!"

"Prejudice never does. But there's no place for it on the soccer field. No place at all." The Colonel looked down at Lucy. "I'll be watching for it tomorrow."

He gave her a sharp nod then and with his hands still in his pockets, he walked away.

Lucy was still standing and staring when he said without turning around, "No matter what happens, play your position."

Lucy was pretty sure he wasn't just talking about soccer.

She was pretty sure he might be an angel.

16

Of all the pep talks Lucy got between then and the opening whistle of the game — Dad's message on the answering machine when she got home Friday — he was out on a "remote" with his class;

Mr. Auggy's final words to the team before the game;

Ms. Pasqual's brief "I'm praying for you" whispered during fourth period; all the pats on the back from the shopkeepers and the cheers from the stands when the Dreams took the field for the warm-up; and even Inez and Mora being right here with them — but very far away from Aunt Karen who sat with Mrs. Cluck and Januarie —

Out of all of them, the thing Lucy thought about most as she tied on her cleats and fastened her shin guards was what the Colonel told her about J.J.'s dad and Coyote Hills. When she'd told Mr. Auggy about it on the way home from ODP practice the night before, he nodded like he was thinking hard.

"J.J. thought that might be part of it," he'd said finally.

"He knew?" Lucy said, and then she rolled her eyes at herself. Of course he knew. The real question was why he hadn't told her.

"Now I want you to focus on what you have ahead of you this weekend," Mr. Auggy said. "And you have a lot."

That was true. And for the first time, Lucy thought it might be more than she could handle. Especially without J.J. He still wasn't giving her more than a grunt or a nod. There was no time to tell him she knew, and maybe Mr. Auggy had done that for her anyway. As she took her place in the center circle, facing Tara and her muscled legs and her hard eyes, Lucy closed her own eyes, just for a tiny second. There was no time for a whole list. Just for a tiny prayer.

"Are you ready?" Ms. Pasqual said.

Lucy was, and from the instant the whistle blew, she gave it her all, and so did the rest of the Dreams. The first half sailed by with no fouls on either side and no Howls passing the ball to J.J. or even looking his way as far as Lucy could tell. In fact, it was as if all the CHKs were wearing masks with no expression on them at all—to hide what Lucy knew was burning behind them.

"Their coach musta threatened them or somethin'," Gabe muttered to Lucy when he passed her to do the throw-in after a Howler kicked the ball out of bounds.

Lucy didn't care what it was. Without all the drama, they could play real soccer. Everything they'd practiced for ODP was suddenly there on the field, and not just in Lucy's game but in Dusty's and Gabe's and J.J.'s. It all kept the ball away from the Dreams' goal and on the Howl's end of the field. Wolf-Man was down on his knee more than he was standing up. By the time the half was nearing, though, the Dreams still hadn't scored. And then a chance opened up.

Wolf-Man had just sent the ball out of the box on the left. Dusty trapped it and looked to Gabe, who at the moment was open. But just as Dusty sent a low pass, Ricky came out of what seemed like no where and went for the ball.

It was right in front of the goal, and there was no one in a position to go for it except Lucy. And there was only one way she was going to make it.

Throw your arms out in front of you and dive toward the ball, she could hear Mr. Auggy saying in her mind. *Meet it with your forehead.*

It was the one soccer move she hated to make.

But she hit the ground and felt the ball smack neatly against her head. She thought the rest of Mr. Auggy's instructions: *get up immediately so you don't get—*

The first blow to her temple came right along with the roar from the crowd. The second kick caught her behind the ear just as someone yelled, "Score!"

After that it was a second—or maybe more—before Lucy heard anything else.

Then it was Ms. Pasqual saying, "Rooney—stay with me. Somebody get the coach!"

The field spun back into itself and Lucy tried to sit up.

"Negative," Ms. Pasqual said.

"I'm fine."

"Good. The five-minute rule still applies. Get her off the field, Coach."

Mr. Auggy squatted in front of her, face white.

"I'm *fine*," Lucy said. "See—I'm not dizzy or anything."

She struggled to her feet and barely wobbled as Coach Auggy led her off the field with his hand under her elbow.

"Sit right here," he said at the bench. "Oscar—play in!"

"You're leaving the goal undefended?" Lucy said, and then she winced.

"Not much going on down there anyway. Look at me."

Lucy stared into Mr. Auggy's face as he searched her eyes.

"Your pupils look good."

"I had a concussion before and this doesn't feel like that," Lucy said. She could hear the begging in her voice. "I can go back in after five minutes, right?"

"You got kicked in the head, Captain."

"Twice."

"Twice?"

"Well, yeah, I mean, with all those feet running around—"

"There was nobody down there but the goalie," Mr. Auggy said. "Show me where you got kicked."

Lucy put her hand to her right temple, and then behind her left ear.

"Okay—we're going to the hospital," someone else said.

Lucy groaned, not from pain but from the sound of Aunt Karen's voice. She was suddenly there on the bench, one hand raking her hair while the other one punched a number on her cell phone.

"I'm not going to the hospital!" Lucy said. "I'm going back in the game!"

"Absolutely not! Sam, if you let her—"

Mr. Auggy put his hand up. "I'm not letting her go back in—"

"What?" Lucy said.

"We can't take a chance with head trauma."

"Not with your tryout tomorrow," Aunt Karen said.

"But there's no reason why she can't watch the rest of the game."

Watch? Her team was out there playing their best ever and Lucy was supposed to *watch?* She thought wildly about red hot tweezers.

"You seriously don't think she needs to go to the emergency room?" Aunt Karen said.

"No," Mr. Auggy said, "I don't."

Okay, so she would watch. If it weren't for Mr. Auggy, she'd be in an ambulance right now.

Aunt Karen rubbed Lucy's head. "You're already getting a lump. I'm going to find you some ice."

"Done." Dusty's mom tucked a cold sandwich bag into Lucy's hand and smiled—a little stiffly—at Aunt Karen.

Lucy held the ice bag to her temple and forgot all of them. The ball was back in play, and her team was spread out, just the way they were supposed to be. Emanuel contained Ricky until he could move in and steal the ball. Gabe received his pass and dribbled until he could get the ball to Dusty. She didn't have the right angle for a shot but she didn't let Skye and Nina get her into a corner.

They were playing like a team—a team with skills and focus. All of them, even Carla Rosa, who was on Tara like a guard dog, and Oscar, who really did know how to do something besides chew on a toothpick.

And in the middle of it all was J.J., shouting calls, "Dusty—man on!" "Gabe—switch the field!"

Quiet, grunting, don't-make-me-talk J.J. at midfield, playing like a captain.

"Through!" he called to Gabe.

From the bench, Lucy saw what he was doing. Nina and Skye were in the perfect position for Gabe to send the ball between them so J.J. could run onto it. He plowed straight to the goal.

And then things seemed to happen at double speed. Wolf-Man came forward to try to catch the ball just as J.J. came in to head it. Wolf-Man reached up to punch it out with his fist. But his curled-up hand never connected with the ball. It landed with a thunk Lucy could hear from the bench, right into J.J.'s eye.

The scene exploded. J.J. and Wolf-Man went to the ground and bodies piled on from all directions—Ricky and Hector and Nina. Mr. Auggy flew from the bench and got himself in front of Gabe and Emanuel and Oscar before they could join in. Although Ms. Pasqual blew her whistle long and hard and over and over, the pile on the ground didn't stop writhing until Mr. Auggy and the Howl coach hauled Ricky and the others off by the backs of their shirts. Even then they pumped their fists in the air and screamed, red-faced, as Ms. Pasqual ordered Wolf-Man and JJ. to their feet.

Lucy came out of her frozen state and lunged for the field, but Aunt Karen's hands closed over her shoulders and pulled her back.

"No, Lucy—you can't help him!" she said.

Only then did Lucy realize she herself was screaming J.J.'s name.

The Howl's coach ordered his team to the other side of the field, and Mr. Auggy did the same with the Dreams. Ms. Pasqual pulled both coaches to her side on the field, and Lucy could see her talking fast and shaking her head.

"I want to go over there with my team," Lucy said to Aunt Karen, who was still holding onto her.

"Lucy—"

"I have to be with my team."

She didn't wait for Aunt Karen to let go. She pulled away and ran to her knot of friends, all huddled and shaken. They couldn't be the same group she'd just seen running the field with their heads high as if they owned it.

Dusty and Veronica were both crying, and Carla Rosa looked ready to be sick. Gabe paced like a dog in a crate. Lucy looked for J.J.

"Hey—she's sayin' somethin'," Oscar said.

The buzzing crowd quieted as Ms. Pasqual held up her arm. She cupped her hands to her mouth and yelled.

"What?" Gabe said.

"I think she said the game's over!" Dusty said. "Lucy—can she do that?"

Lucy didn't answer. She was searching the bench, the field, the stands, for J.J.

And he was nowhere.

17

Lucy heard the voices—Dusty's, Aunt Karen's, Mr. Auggy's—all crying and shrieking and calling to her to stop, but she left them in the dust she kicked up as she tore frantically behind the bleachers and down the dirt driveway. Her head throbbed with pain and thoughts.

J.J. couldn't run away again. Children's Services would find him. They'd put him in foster care.

But he couldn't stay here either. He'd gotten in a fight, and they would put him in foster care for that, too.

He was like a hamster, running around in a cage, and Lucy felt as if she was trapped in one, too, as she cried out his name until her throat croaked, and squinted beyond the cacti as far as the Sacramentos. But there was no J.J.

She had to stop at the bridge and grope for her breath. But when she heard a car approaching behind her, she started off again. She couldn't handle Aunt Karen right now. She just couldn't.

Gravel popped under the car's tires as it slowed down, and a horn beeped. A Jeep horn.

"Get in, Miss Lucy," Mr. Auggy said out the window. "Let's find J.J."

They didn't talk as Lucy climbed in and Mr. Auggy drove it at a crawl—across the bridge, up and down the narrow streets and back across the highway. Lucy sat up on her knees, head out in the wind, searching behind every cottonwood, around every elder tree, inside every shop on Granada Street.

Mr. Auggy, she knew, was looking just as hard from his side of the car, and when they pulled up beside Lucy's house, where only Mudge waited by the gate, her coach's face was as pinched and pasty as she was sure hers was.

"Do we have to stop looking?" she said. "We could try the school—and the desert."

"I will," Mr. Auggy said. He seemed older now than he had this morning. "We haven't sorted all this out yet, what happened down there on the field. We have to hear J.J.'s side of it, but it doesn't look good for him."

Lucy turned from him and looked at J.J.'s house—the house that had just started to look like a place where a person could live.

"J.J. was doing so well before we met those Coyote Hills kids," she said. "Why did all this have to happen now and ruin it?"

"I don't know, Captain, but we have to deal with it."

His voice was almost stern, not like the sound of a Jeep horn at all. Lucy kept her eyes away, on J.J.'s house.

"If you find him, or if he comes to you, you have to tell me where he is."

Lucy got up on her knee again and scooted toward the windshield. Had she seen something move in J.J.'s window, or was she just wishing?

"They're not automatically going to put him in foster care," Mr. Auggy said. "We just need to talk to him."

"Then you'd better go to his house." Lucy pointed a finger that was shaky with relief. "Because that's where he is."

"The sheriff already checked there, Captain."

"I just saw him in his window."

"Seriously?"

Lucy nodded as once again a hand made a vent in the sheet over his window, and J.J.'s dark head appeared like a blink in the triangle of light before he folded out of sight.

All the air seemed to go out of Mr. Auggy. Lucy didn't even try to fight her tears.

"Let me make a call," Mr. Auggy said, picking up his cell phone. "And then the J-Man and I have some talking to do."

But J.J. wasn't talking. Aunt Karen announced that when she came back from taking Mrs. Cluck home.

"Mr. Auggy says he's locked himself in his room. He won't even open up for *him.*" She perched on the edge of the Napping Couch where she had Lucy propped up with two ice bags on her head under the threat of permanent groundation if she moved. Lucy felt far too heavy and sad to argue. The news about J.J. drove her even further into the pillows.

"You probably won't believe this," Aunt Karen said, "but I suggested that maybe he'd talk to you. I mean, the boy obviously has it bad for you."

Lucy didn't know what that meant. She just shook her head. "He doesn't want to talk to me."

"Ah. I see." Aunt Karen gave Lucy's ankle a squeeze. "I'm sorry—I really am. That first heartbreak can be so painful. There are going to be a lot of other boys in your life, but your first love will always be with you."

Lucy closed her eyes. Maybe if she pretended to be asleep, all the things Aunt Karen didn't understand would go away. Or at least maybe Aunt Karen would.

"That's exactly what you need to do—rest," Aunt Karen said. "Tomorrow is the really important day. That's the one that counts."

Today counted. It counted so much it ached inside her.

"I want to talk to my dad," Lucy said.

"We can try calling him, but he said he was going to be on that remote deal out of cell phone range until late. You're going to see him tomorrow anyway." Aunt Karen squeezed her ankle again. "Come on—let's get you bathed and fed and in your own bed. I'm making you a protein shake. Your electrolytes are probably completely out of whack. Nutrition and a good night's sleep are what you need."

Lucy was sure she would never go to sleep, since that was *not* what she needed. But after the shake she drank just to hush Aunt Karen up, and the hot bath with some kind of oils swimming around in it, and a long, lonely stare out of her window at J.J.'s until the sun hissed out behind the mountains—after all of that Lucy did turn out her light and wound up tight under the covers with Lolli purring around her head.

Number One, she thought, because she was too weary to talk to God out loud. *Please. Just—please.*

She was even too tired to think. And so she listened. Somewhere at a gray edge that curled softly about her she felt a thought about letting go and peace on earth and treasuring things she only just now knew...

She awoke with a start as Lollipop startled from the pillow and leaped to the windowsill. Lucy rolled over and made out the numbers on her clock.

"It's three in the morning, Lolli," Lucy mumbled. "What are you doing?"

Something pinged on the window and Lolli pawed at the glass and Lucy knew what had bounced her out of sleep. Not daring to hope, she scrambled to the window and looked into the half-moonlit night. There was no silhouette of J.J. in his yard or at his window.

"We were only hoping, Lolli," Lucy whispered.

And then she gasped as a faced popped up just inches from the glass.

"J.J.!"

J.J. put his finger to his lips and held up something square and flat. It was her Book of Lists.

"Back steps," Lucy mouthed to him.

And without giving him a chance to refuse, she crept out of her room, forcing herself to move slowly. Down the hall, Aunt Karen's light was off and her door was closed. There wasn't a sound except for Mr. Auggy's voice in her mind's ear, telling her all the way to the back door: *We have to deal with it. If he comes to you, you have to—*

Lucy turned the doorknob and watched Marmalade, asleep on Dad's kitchen chair, to make sure he wasn't going to wake up and holler for food and give her away. His orange belly moved up and down in soft rhythm.

Lucy slid out into the chilly night and immediately wished she'd grabbed a sweatshirt. But J.J. was there, standing with his foot on the bottom steps as if he were going to spring from it any minute, and she didn't know how long she could keep him there.

"I brought your book," he said before Lucy even got to him.

"I didn't know you had it," Lucy said.

"Mora told me to keep it for you."

"Oh."

"She said if she kept it, she'd read it."

"Probably."

"So—I guess—here."

J.J. stuck the book out, but Lucy didn't take it. The minute she did, he wouldn't have a reason to keep standing there.

"Could we sit down?" she said. "My head hurts."

Which was true. It felt like someone had kicked her again while she was sleeping. "I gotta go," J.J. said, but he dropped to the step anyway.

Lucy made herself sit, made her words come out calm and slow —not frightened and grabby like they wanted to.

"Where are you going?" she said.

"Away."

"Is that why you brought my book to me in the middle of the night?"

"I didn't want your aunt to see it."

"Thanks," Lucy said.

"Hide it good."

"J.J.—where's 'away'—where are you going?"

"Can't tell you."

"They'll find you—and then you'll be in more trouble." Lucy looked up at the back window, but no light went on in Aunt Karen's room. Lucy brought her voice down. "Mr. Auggy says they won't automatically put you in foster care for fighting."

"It wasn't my fault."

"Then just tell the truth. Mr. Auggy says you can help them sort it out."

J.J. leaned back on the steps, into the porch light, and Lucy saw that his left eye was purple and swollen almost shut. It made her own face ache even more.

"They won't believe me."

"Why not?"

"You don't know."

"Yes, I do. It's because of your dad, because he came from Coyote Hills and he can't go back."

J.J. didn't answer. He didn't have to. His jaw did it for him.

"So we'll tell Mr. Auggy we won't play the Howl any more. And at school—"

"It's never gonna be different." J.J.'s voice shot up so high, Lucy barely heard the last word. "My dad's gone—but he's still here."

He thumped his chest with his fist. Lucy shook her head but he kept punching himself until Lucy reached out and grabbed his hand. J.J. shook it off and stood up. The Book of Lists tumbled from his lap and onto the ground.

"Sorry," J.J. said.

He picked it up and brushed it off and held it out to Lucy. She looked at it and shook her head.

"What?" he said.

"If you're going to run away, you'd better take that with you."

The words were out of her mouth before she knew she thought them.

"Why?" J.J. said. "It's your book. You need it."

"No—you need it. Because if you run, they'll find you before you even get down Granada Street—because when you go out the gate, I'm calling Mr. Auggy."

J.J.'s eyes were stunned.

"It's not right and I won't help you—even though you're my best friend in the world even when you're mad at me for trying to protect you." Lucy took a breath that was ragged with tears. "I was wrong to do that, so now I'm not doing it. You have to fight for yourself, only not like your dad does. You can't run away just because you're scared of yourself."

Her words tangled on J.J.'s face. Lucy knew she wasn't making sense to him. She didn't know what *did* make sense—except for one thing.

J.J. was still holding the Book out to her. Lucy pushed it into his chest.

"If you run, they'll find you, and you *will* go to a foster home then, and you won't have anybody to talk to except God. And this—" she pointed to her Book—"is how you talk to God, and you'd better, J.J., because God's the only one who gets it all the time."

J.J.'s thumb moved over the raised gold leaves on the book's cover.

"I can't write," he said.

"It's not really writing. It's lists."

"Lists."

"God lists." Lucy took a breath. "I'll show you."

The words came out on their own again. She'd never invited anyone to look at her lists. She was breaking every Dad-rule to keep them private. But her heart rose from that low place it had sunk to as J.J. sat back down on the step and handed her the Book—as she opened it to the first page, written so many months ago now, what she'd said to God before she even knew it was God she was talking to. Before Inez had told her.

"Why I Wish Aunt Karen Would Move to Australia," she read out loud.

J.J. grunted a laugh at that one. He nodded at others. Over some he swallowed hard as Lucy read with tears close to her voice.

Lucy read until light peeked over the fence and Mudge yowled for his breakfast and the last page was turned. Then J.J. put the Book in Lucy's hands.

"I can't take it," he said. He looked at her crooked from the sides of his eyes. "I gotta get my own."

"Okay," Lucy said.

J.J. almost smiled and Lucy almost cried and then he ambled to the gate with his lanky arms flopping at his sides. He was just closing it behind him when Aunt Karen flung the back door open.

"My word! Was that J.J.?"

"Yes," Lucy said.

"Where's he going? Grab him, Lucy—no, I'll grab him."

"You don't have to grab him," Lucy said. "He's going home."

18

Once Aunt Karen made sure J.J. was in his house—just like Lucy *told* her—she went at making a protein shake as if the ingredients needed to be disciplined, ranting the entire time.

"You stayed up half the night before the biggest day of your life so far—what were you thinking? You *weren't* thinking, that's the problem. I don't see how you're going to make any kind of showing at the tryouts—you *will* sleep all the way up there if I have to tape your eyelids closed—"

Lucy didn't need tape for her eyelids. They closed just fine as she rested her head on her arms on the kitchen table. When they opened again, Marmalade was curled up in her lap, and Mr. Auggy was sitting across the table from her. There wasn't a small smile within a hundred miles.

"I think J.J.'s going to cooperate now," Lucy said.

"I just talked to him," Mr. Auggy said. "Whatever you said to him, I'm glad you did. He's moving in the right direction. There's still a lot to be worked out—he did get into a fight. We'll see."

"So can you focus on you now, Lucy?" Aunt Karen said from the counter.

Mr. Auggy put a hand up without turning around to look at her. She folded her arms and leaned against the sink and frowned an eleven wrinkle between her eyebrows.

"Look at me, Miss Lucy," Mr. Auggy said.

Lucy did, and he studied her face.

"How does your head feel?"

"It hurts a little bit."

He waited.

"Okay, it feels like somebody stepped on me."

"Somebody did," Aunt Karen said. "And if that interferes with her chances for ODP, I *will* be talking to that boy's parents."

Mr. Auggy sat back in his chair and slathered his face with his hand. "Captain," he said, "a no-show is better than a bad show. If I take you to Albuquerque today, in the condition you're in, you'll probably still perform better than the average soccer player. But that isn't enough."

"I have to be elite."

"And I guarantee you won't be today."

"Not even if I stuff her full of vitamins and make her sleep all the way there?" Aunt Karen said.

Mr. Auggy shook his head.

"You're saying that's it? She just doesn't try out?" Aunt Karen pulled her hand so hard through her hair, Lucy expected it all to come out. "I just don't think that's a smart move. Sam, you're not even giving this a chance."

He didn't take his eyes from Lucy. "It isn't up to me. It's up to the Captain."

Lucy sank back in her chair. Not try out for ODP — after all the high hopes, and the hard work — hers and her friends' — and all the disappointments she'd had to overcome? Just give up on the dream she had painted in her lists — the dream of being like Mom, and maybe better so that wherever she was, Mom would be proud? All because she'd helped her best friend?

She ran her palm over Marmalade, who was still purring like a motor in her lap, and waited for the knot in her stomach and the tears in her throat and the urge to yell, "It's not fair!" But none of that came. She only knew that Mr. Auggy was right.

"You know that promise I made you?" she said.

"What promise?" Aunt Karen said.

Mr. Auggy nodded. "The one where you said you'd tell me if you ever wanted to stop for any reason."

"Well," Lucy said. "I'm keeping it."

Aunt Karen smacked her hands on the counter. "Lucy! I'm not going to let you do this!"

"You're sure?" Mr. Auggy said to Lucy.

"I can't play my best today," Lucy said.

"Even your worst is better than other people's best!"

Lucy looked closer at her aunt. That tone Lucy heard—that couldn't be coming from her. Aunt Karen never sounded like she believed in somebody so much it hurt right through her voice.

Mr. Auggy fished his cell phone out of his pocket and poked in some numbers and said, "Hey, Fred—Sam Augustalientes. We have a situation here with Lucy Rooney."

He didn't leave the room like most grown-ups would and murmur the conversation in a no-hear zone. In quiet words he told a story that must have happened to someone else. A story about a girl named Lucy who had dealt with weeks of tension and teasing and dirty playing and even a head injury, with a sense of integrity beyond her years. Who had led her team to a victory not of points but of character. And who had sat up with a friend whose safety was in danger, so that she was in no shape to compete in a tryout today.

Lucy was still wondering if all of that was really true, when Mr. Auggy handed her the phone.

"Coach Yancey wants to talk to you," he said.

Lucy half-whispered a hello.

"Lucy, I'm going to give it to you straight," the crispy voice said. "I understand you're a phenomenal player and after seeing your video I tend to agree. We'd like to give you an opportunity to work with the program, so we will extend your application until our next tryouts in the spring."

"Really?" Lucy said. "I can do that?"

"What?" Aunt Karen whispered. "What can you do?"

"But let me say this." Coach Yancey's voice became even crisper. "If you have your sights set on the Olympics, soccer has to come before everything else in your life. That's something to think about in the next six months."

Lucy somehow managed to say good-bye and handed the phone to Mr. Auggy. She pulled Marmalade up to her face and let the tears squeeze out into his orange fur.

"So what's the deal?" Aunt Karen said.

Mr. Auggy didn't seem to hear her. "You okay, Captain?" he said.

"I really wanted to see my Dad today," Lucy said. She had to blink hard to see him. "I'm going outside—by myself."

Aunt Karen seemed to get that because she didn't follow Lucy with a protein shake and a lecture about how Lucy should have gone to the tryouts with her achy head and her tired muscles and given it everything she had.

Everything.

Lucy sat down on the steps where she and J.J. had talked for hours in the starlight and watched Artemis Hamm stalk her way along the top of the fence. If what Coach Yancey said was true, then did getting to the Olympics, even getting into the ODP, meant eating like a health nut rabbit instead of enjoying a grilled cheese at Felix Pasco's? And making friends like Veronica and Carla Rosa and Oscar and Emanuel feel like they weren't good enough to practice with her? Did it mean letting J.J. run away scared if that was what he got into his head—just so she would be ready for what was expected of her?

Six months was a long time to think about it. But after six minutes, she already knew she couldn't make a decision yet. All she wanted to do right now was sleep.

Her room was late-afternoon dark when Lollipop woke her up, pawing at the door to get out.

"I'll feed you in a minute," Lucy said. "Just let me get my eyes open."

Lolli gave an insistent meow. But that wasn't the only voice Lucy heard. Someone else was talking in the kitchen, and it sounded like—

Lucy was down the hall before she could even get the word "Dad!" out of her mouth. Even when she threw her arms around him in the kitchen she didn't dare believe he was real. Only when she breathed in the Dad-smells of breath mints and tweedy jacket—only when he said, "Hey, Champ," did she know.

And then she cried and cried until all the bad was out and there was only her and Dad on the Sitting Couch with three cats. That was when she finally asked him how he got there.

"Mr. Auggy drove up to Albuquerque and brought me back," he said.

"But what about school?" Lucy's stomach knotted. "If you don't go you'll get fired and that'll be because of me—"

"Luce, Luce. First of all, I know you've taken responsibility for everyone in town while I was gone, but you are not responsible for whether I lose my job." He scratched behind Marmalade's ear. "They've given me a few days off to get some things worked out here."

"Some things like Inez?" Lucy said.

Dad nodded. "Let's start there. Why don't you tell me how you saw it?"

She did. And he listened. And slowly the knots in Lucy's stomach untied.

The room was afternoon dim when she finished and she was ready to curl up on the Napping Couch. As Dad was tucking her in and running his hand over her face the way he did when he wanted to look at her, he stopped.

"I feel a worry," he said. "Come on—no holding back, Luce."

Lucy swallowed hard. "I was just wondering—"

"Yeah?"

"Do you think Mom would be upset that I decided not to go for the ODP? I mean—" She felt her voice break. "Would she still be proud of me?"

Dad sat down on the couch beside her. "Oh, Champ," he said, and his voice broke, too. Right in half. "Your mom would be proud of you no matter what you did, because you have held onto you and you've held onto God."

"Does doing the right thing always feel this horrible?" Lucy was crying so hard now she could hardly get the words out.

"How horrible does it feel?" Dad said.

"Like I'm being torn in half."

She let herself cry, and she waited for Dad to tell her that was the way growing up was, and that soon her whole self would come back together.

But he stayed quiet for a long time. And when he spoke, his voice was almost softer than the silence.

"I can't teach you how to make decisions and then not let you make them," he said. "But I don't want you to make *this* one without hearing this."

Lucy got up on her elbows. "What?" she said.

"Everything worth having in this life is worth making a sacrifice for. Your mom knew that. You know it, too. But God never asks us to sacrifice who He made us to be."

"Am I just soccer?"

"You are everything a person has to be in order to be a great soccer player—and it isn't just about the skills."

Lucy started to cry again. "I'm so confused, Dad."

"I know the feeling." He gave his sandpapery chuckle. "I'm the father of a twelve year old girl."

He stood up and motioned for Lucy to snuggle back in so he could cover her up again.

"Did Mom ever get confused?" Lucy said.

This time Dad didn't chuckle. He smiled his sunlight smile, even though it was a little watery. "She was never confused when it came to you," he said.

"I wish she was here."

"She is. In a heart that's exactly like hers. Exactly."

✳

Even people who could have cared less about soccer were talking about the game at school Monday. Lucy and the team spent the whole day snuffing out the rumors that flared up like brush fires all over the place—everything from 'Lucy has brain damage from being kicked in the head by the entire Coyote Hills team' to 'Wolf-Man is lucky somebody pulled J.J. off him because J.J. has a black belt in karate.'

"Where do they get this stuff?" Dusty said at lunch, after the

Queen B's stopped at the Dreams' table to announce that they heard the Howl coach and Mr. Auggy were going to fight each other on the soccer field at midnight.

"They make it up," Veronica said. "And I'm so over them."

"Guess what?" Carla Rosa said. "I was always over them."

But there was still one rumor Lucy couldn't just toss water on, because she was afraid it was true. J.J. had said that morning on the way to school that even though he'd told Mr. Auggy everything that had happened on the soccer field, it was still his word against Wolf-Man's, and Wolf-Man's parents were threatening to press charges against him. Children's Services wouldn't be happy about that.

Lucy's heart was practically dragging the ground again when she got to sixth period. It didn't help that the Colonel took J.J. out into the hall while the rest of them were taking a quiz. J.J. didn't need to be failing math on top of everything else. It was hard to stop being protective of him. Maybe she didn't have to give up *all* of that.

When J.J. came back in, somebody — not Wolf-Man or Ricky — said, "Busted," but J.J. didn't look as if he'd just been "busted" at all. He had a hopeful gleam in his good eye when he told Lucy the Colonel wanted to see her next.

The Colonel was sending some wandering kid packing when Lucy got there. He shook his head.

"There's always somebody who has to push the envelope," he said. "Kids like you and J.J. are a breath of fresh air."

"We are?" Lucy said.

"Saw your game Saturday." He peered closely at Lucy. "You don't look too much the worse for wear, considering the beating you took. I'm sorry, but I couldn't tell whether you were kicked on purpose or it was just an accident of play."

"That's okay," Lucy said. "J.J.'s the one I'm worried about."

"Now, that one I did see. And now that I've discussed it with J.J. I'm going to talk to the sheriff this afternoon."

"The sheriff?" Lucy said.

"He needs to know that Wolfgang threw the first punch, and it was intentional, no doubt about that. That boy needs to be reined in, or we will have another Ian Cluck on our hands. I don't want to see a second soccer program go down."

Lucy felt her eyes widen. "Is that what happened way back then? They stopped soccer because of J.J.'s dad?"

The Colonel nodded. "For fifteen years. It's only now coming back to life and I want to see it stay that way. I need your help with that if you're willing."

"I don't think Wolf-Man would listen to me," Lucy said. J.J. was one thing, but—

"Not by yourself. Ms. Pasqual and I are forming an anti-bullying council and we agree that you should be involved."

"You sure you want me?" Lucy said. "They call me the Class Weirdo."

"That's the number one requirement," the Colonel said. "Oh, and by the way—I'm sure Ted Rooney is very proud of you."

And then he smiled.

But Lucy didn't smile back.

"Something wrong?" he said.

"Not exactly. I just have a question."

"And that would be?"

"If we're gonna stop people from bullying and make soccer a clean sport so we don't have to be afraid of getting our heads kicked in—" Lucy cut herself off to take a huge breath. The Colonel seemed to be listening like she was a grown-up. "If we're going to do that, what's it going to take?"

He didn't even stop to think. "A great deal of sacrifice—of time, of being considered cool. And it's going to take heart. Lots of it."

He smiled a second time. "And that you have, Lucy Rooney."

Lucy ran most of the way home from school so she wouldn't lose a minute of her time with Dad. He was sitting at the table, eating one of Inez's *sopapillas*. Inez was at the stove, stirring what smelled like heaven, but was probably her enchilada sauce. Even Mora was in her usual place, poking at her cell phone with her thumbs.

"Are you back?" Lucy said.

"We're not a figment of your imagination," Mora said without looking up.

"I mean, for good?"

"For very good," Inez said.

"Just one of the things I needed to work out," Dad said with his sunlight smile.

Lucy wondered if the other one was Aunt Karen, whose car wasn't parked outside, but the moment was too perfect to bring her up.

"Are we going to finish our Bible study?" she said instead.

"It's only Monday," Mora said.

"I think you already learn what Senora Mary has to teach," Inez said.

"Do I get to hear what that is?" Dad said. "Or is this strictly a girl thing?"

"It is woman-thing." Inez wiped her hands on her apron and folded them on the back of the chair where she had sat so many times with her Bible and its skin-like-an-onion pages. "The last test to pass to begin to become a woman, you have passed, Senorita Lucy. You now do what Senora Mary did."

She wasn't going to tell what that was, of course. She was going to make Lucy figure it out herself, and Lucy had to search back through all that had happened in a short, intense time to find it. But it was there.

"She let God do his thing," she said, "and she treasured it all in her heart."

"Ah," Dad said. "Surrender."

"Isn't that like when you're about to get arrested?" Mora said.

Lucy was pretty sure that wasn't what Dad meant, but right then she decided that even if God arrested her, she'd be okay with that.

✳

STUFF I'M TREASURING, GOD,

she wrote later in her Book of Lists

1. Making a decision to stay here and be on the bully squad and keep soccer going and not let prejudice destroy the beautiful game.
2. Sacrifices that don't make me feel like I'm being ripped in half.
3. Sacrifices that make me feel like my mom.

She was on a roll, but before she could write down number four, there was a tap on her door.

"Come in, Dad," Lucy said.

But it was Aunt Karen who poked her head in. If Lucy didn't know better she'd say her eyes were scared.

"Don't worry," Lucy said. "Lollipop's not in here."

"It isn't the cat I'm afraid of," Aunt Karen said. "It's you."

Lucy slowly put her pen down. "I don't get it," she said.

"Is it all right if I come in?"

Okay, something was very strange here. Lucy nodded and made a space on the bed for her to sit, but she felt her tummy tightening up again.

"Your dad and I have been talking," Aunt Karen said as she parked carefully on the edge. "He has to go back to school for two more weeks, and Inez has agreed to come and stay with you for that short time. I'm sure that makes you happy."

In fact, Lucy did want to cheer. But that yearning thing was in Aunt Karen's voice again that made her wait to hear more.

"Before I leave though, I really want to tell you something."

Okay. As long as this was the last make-over lecture she ever had to listen to.

Aunt Karen looked at the ceiling. "I've tried so hard with you,

Lucy. I've bought you things most girls would kill to have. I've offered you a great education, a better home — "

"There is no better home than this one."

"See, that's what I didn't understand." Aunt Karen shook her head. "You and your father barely have a nickel to your names. You have almost as much responsibility as I do and you're only eleven years old. I wanted to relieve you of all that, and yet all I've done is make you think I'm some kind of ogre."

Lucy wasn't exactly sure what an ogre was, but she didn't think it was anything like the lady with the confused eyes and the wiggly lip who sagged at the end of Lucy's bed and actually looked like she was going to cry.

"But now I think I know why I can't change your life," Aunt Karen said. "Because you are just exactly like your mother, and I couldn't change hers either."

Lucy stared. "Why did you want to make her life different?"

"Because I was so afraid. What she did as a reporter was dangerous, and I didn't want to lose her." The words seemed to catch on something in her throat. "And I did, Lucy. I lost my sister."

For a moment Lucy didn't think she knew what to say. But as she watched Aunt Karen lick away the tears that straggled to her lips, she did know.

"And now you don't want to lose me?" she said.

Aunt Karen dabbed at the sunken places under her eyes. "I know you don't get that — "

But Lucy was nodding. "Yes I do. It's like, I tried to protect J.J. all the time, too, and I just made it worse. It's a lot better since I started letting God do his thing." She shrugged. "Dad calls that surrender but Mora says it sounds like somebody's being arrested — so you could probably just think of it like God's better at everything than us."

Tears were still trickling down Aunt Karen's face and her nose was running, too, which was something you *never* saw. But the sound coming out of her throat wasn't crying. She was laughing, giggling like Veronica on her best day.

"What's funny?" Lucy said.

"Nothing," Aunt Karen. "What you are seeing is pure delight, Lucy. Please — will you let me know who you are?" She put up both hands— like she was surrendering. "I don't *want* to change you any more. Why would I want anything different from what I'm seeing right here in front of me? You are like having my sister right here with me."

Lucy could only stare as Aunt Karen stood up. "Well, I just wanted to say that. I'm going to go over and say good-bye to Anita."

"Don't say good-bye," Lucy said.

"I have to. We've gotten close."

"No, I mean, don't go. Stay here."

Aunt Karen blinked her blue eyes. "You mean, with you?"

"I can do anything for two more weeks," Lucy said. She sat straight up. "Just one thing you have to know about me first, though."

"What?" Aunt Karen said.

Lucy felt herself grin. "Lucy Rooney doesn't wear pink."

"Okay," Aunt Karen said. Lucy was pretty sure she was crying when she left.

As her tappy heels faded down the hallway, Lucy sank back against her giant stuffed soccer ball with her Book of Lists and picked up her pen.

STUFF I'M TREASURING, GOD,

she'd written. Now, for number four...

But she closed the Book and hugged it to her chest. The rest of the list would be so long, she could be here for the rest of her life.

"Thanks for the Book, Mom," she whispered. "But I think I know how to be a girl now."

A Lucy Novel
Bestselling author Nancy Rue

Lucy Rooney is a feisty, precocious tomboy who questions everything — even God. It's not hard to see why: a horrible accident killed her mother and blinded her father, turning her life upside down. It will take a strong but gentle housekeeper — who insists on Bible study and homework when all Lucy wants to do is play soccer — to show Lucy that there are many ways to become the woman God intends her to be.

BOOK 1: Lucy Doesn't Wear Pink

BOOK 3: Lucy's "Perfect" Summer

BOOK 2: Lucy Out of Bounds

BOOK 4: Lucy Finds Her Way

Sophie Series
Written by Nancy Rue

Meet Sophie LaCroix, a creative soul with a desire to become a great film director someday, and she definitely has a flair for drama! Her overactive imagination frequently lands her in trouble, but her faith and friends always save the day. Each bind-up includes two books in one.

Sophie and Friends
Includes *Sophie's First Dance* and *Sophie's Stormy Summer!*

Sophie Flakes Out
Includes *Sophie Flakes Out* and *Sophie Loves Jimmy!*

Sophie Steps Up
Includes *Sophie Under Pressure* and *Sophie Steps Up!*

Sophie's Drama
Includes *Sophie's Drama* and *Sophie Gets Real!*

Sophie's Friendship Fiasco
Includes *Sophie's Friendship Fiasco* and *Sophie and the New Girl!*

Available in stores and online!

Boarding School Mysteries
Written by Kristi Holl

The Boarding School Mysteries series challenges twelve-year-old Jeri McKane, a sixth grader at the private Landmark School for Girls, to trust God's Word and direction as this amateur sleuth searches for clues in the midst of danger.

Vanished
(*Formerly titled* Fading Tracks)

Burned
(*Formerly titled* Smoke Screen)

Betrayed
(*Formerly titled* Secrets for Sale)

Poisoned
(*Formerly titled* Pick Your Poison)

Every girl wants to know she's totally unique and special.
This Bible says that with Faithgirlz! sparkle!
Now girls can grow closer to God as they discover the journey
of a lifetime, in their language, for their world.

The NIV Faithgirlz! Bible

Hardcover
Softcover

The NKJV Faithgirlz! Bible

The NIV Faithgirlz! Backpack Bible

Turquoise
Italian Duo-Tone™

Available now at your local bookstore!
Visit www.faithgirlz.com. It's the place for girls ages 9–12.

ZONDERkidz™

101 Ways to Have Fun
Things You Can Do with Friends, Anytime!

In today's world, a girl's free time is precious, but figuring out how to make the most of those spare moments can sometimes be difficult. Faithgirlz! is here to help, with over one hundred unique ideas, activities, and time maximizers you can do by yourself or with your friends. From planning the perfect relaxing afternoon to creating quick and awesome DIY masterpieces, and even tips on hosting amazing sleepovers (complete with lip synch battles and the best-ever snacks), 101 Ways to Have Fun has something for every situation and mood. Whether you have ten minutes or an entire afternoon to fill, finding the ultimate ways to de-stress and kick back with friends has never been easier!

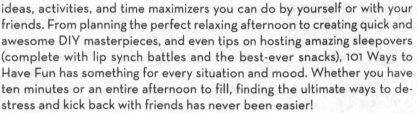

101 Things Every Girl Should Know
Expert Advice on Stuff Big and Small

The editors of Faithgirlz! and Girls' Life have collected their best advice to help girls take charge and feel confident in a variety of situations, from changing a bike tire to talking to your teacher about a bad grade, from being threatened by a bully to falling down the stairs at school. What do you do when you're at a party and you don't know anyone? What's the formal way to set a table (and why does it matter)? This random collection of problem-solving strategies helps with everyday stuff, big and small. With tips, advice, and lots of humor, this is a book every girl needs.

Available in stores and online!

Best Hair Book Ever!

Cute Cuts, Sweet Styles and Tons of
Tress Tips

Buh-bye, bad hair days! This complete guide to care,
cuts and cute styles makes it easy to have amazing
hair each and every day of the week. With tons of
tutorials for pretty ponies, bold braids and easy updos, you'll go from school to
sports to sleepovers with your loveliest-ever locks.

Plus, get the answers to your trickiest tress troubles: How do you fix frizz
once and for all? What's the best way to get tousled curls or an awesome blow-
out? What are the secrets to growing out your hair...fast? All these answers
(and more) inside this girly guide filled with tried 'n' true tips and techniques.

So no matter what your strand-styling skill level is now, you'll soon be the girl
who's showing her friends how to finesse a fishtail or do a double Dutch braid.
And what's more beautiful than that?

Redo Your Room

50 Bedroom DIYs You Can Do in a
Weekend

Whether you're looking for an all-out room redo or a
few new tricks to brighten up your space, Faithgirlz!
has tons easy how-tos and quick DIYs that'll morph
your room into a true expression of y-o-u. Give your
walls a burst of color (even without a bucket of paint!)
and turn your fave pics and keepsakes into inspiring
art. These floor-to-ceiling secrets help nix those piles of clothes decorating
your space in favor of awesome add-ons, like mini murals and a magical ribbon
chandelier (psst: we won't tell anyone it took you a half hour to whip up).

Redo Your Room is packed with cute and crafty ways to add pop to your
domain. You'll learn how to make even the tiniest spaces into pretty places to
sleep 'n' study, and clever ways to keep it all looking adorable. And the best
part? You can make over your bedroom without going broke.

Available in stores and online!